You can return this item to any library but please
note that not all libraries are open every day.
Items must be returned on or before the due date.
Failure to do so will result in overdue charges.
Items may be renewed unless requested by
another customer, in person or by telephone, on
two occasions only. Your membership card number
will be required.
Please look after this item – you may be charged
for any damage.

Headquarters:
Information, Culture & Community Learning,
Town Hall, Bournemouth BH2 6DY

Bournemouth
Libraries

IN A WELSH VALLEY

When Ruth Greene's cousin Dora has to go into hospital, Ruth's family rallies round by going to look after the grocery shop she runs in her Welsh mining village in Carmarthenshire. This gives them a respite from the London blitz, but other dangers and excitements await them in their temporary home. Young Basil gets into mischief, while their daughter, Marina, falls in love for the first time. But can her wartime love endure?

CATRIONA McCUAIG

IN A WELSH VALLEY

Complete and Unabridged

LINFORD
Leicester

First published in Great Britain in 2007

First Linford Edition
published 2008

British Library CIP Data

McCuaig, Catriona
  In a Welsh valley.—Large print ed.—
Linford romance library
  1. World War, *1939 – 1945*—Wales—
Camarthenshire—Fiction
  2. Camarthenshire (Wales)—Fiction
  3. Love stories 4. Large type books
  I. Title
  823.9'2 [F]

  ISBN 978–1–84782–151–5

Published by
F. A. Thorpe (Publishing)
Anstey, Leicestershire

Set by Words & Graphics Ltd.
Anstey, Leicestershire
Printed and bound in Great Britain by
T. J. International Ltd., Padstow, Cornwall

A Cry For Help

It was Monday morning and Ruth Greene looked with despair at the huge pile of washing. The last thing she wanted — after a restless night in the Anderson shelter — was to have to tackle the weekly wash.

As she sorted the whites from the coloureds and put them into the copper to boil, Ruth realised — with a sigh of annoyance — that she'd left her nightie upstairs.

Unfortunately she couldn't make it do for another week. Down in the shelter last night, a particularly loud explosion had made her jump and she'd splashed tea all over herself, and everyone knew that tea made an almost permanent stain if you didn't wash it out right away; she'd even heard of women trying to dye their hair with it.

'Oh, dear, somebody's getting it,'

young Basil had remarked when the noise of the explosion had faded away.

He'd sounded so like his father that Ruth had smiled. But her smile had soon faded; Bob had been out and about on his Home Guard duties, and could well have been in the thick of it somewhere in the town.

Ruth's neighbour had said to her recently, 'I think I'd rather be in London when the raids are on. I bet it would be fun, sleeping down the Tube with everyone else, having a bit of a sing-song and sharing a Thermos of tea. At least having a laugh would take your mind off what was going on outside.'

But Ruth thought that her neighbour was a very silly woman. Even though London wasn't very far away, things were much worse there than in Hertfordshire.

Ruth turned her thoughts back to the present as she trudged up the stairs to the main bedroom, which was such a mess that no amount of tidying up could do much to improve it. The

window was covered with chicken wire
— to prevent flying glass in case of blast
— and in addition to the marital bed,
two camp beds had been crammed into
the room.

Under normal circumstances, Basil
and his elder sister, Marina, had their
own rooms, but since the raids had
become heavier and more frequent,
Ruth had insisted that they all stay
together at night.

Marina had moaned about this
arrangement, of course, complaining
that Basil talked in his sleep and kept
her awake. But Ruth was adamant.
Whenever the sirens sounded and they
needed to get down to the shelter in a
hurry, then she wanted no running
about in the dark wondering where
everybody was.

Hearing the creak of the garden gate,
she peered through the wire on the
window to see a young chap in RAF
uniform carefully propping his bicycle
against the garden wall.

She frowned. What on earth could he

want? Surely Marina hadn't got herself involved with some boy; not after all her father's warnings about sixteen being too young for that sort of thing.

If this one was coming to ask Bob's permission to take the girl to a dance or to the pictures, then he needn't bother. He'd be sent away with a flea in his ear.

Ruth ran downstairs and opened the door, thinking that the young man standing awkwardly beside the pile of sand bags looked vaguely familiar. Perhaps she'd come across him on her volunteer days at the servicemen's canteen.

'Auntie Ruth?' The boy hesitated, his forehead creased. 'It's me, Ifor.'

Ruth's hand flew to her mouth. 'Goodness me, you've grown!' she exclaimed.

What a stupid thing to say! Of course he'd grown; she hadn't seen him since he was a small boy and now he was old enough to join the services!

'Come on in, Ifor, and I'll put the kettle on.' Ruth shepherded the boy into the house. 'You mustn't look at the mess; I'm in the middle of washday, as you can see.'

'I'm sorry to turn up on your doorstep like this, Auntie, but there wasn't time to write. I'm stationed not too far from here and I was lucky to be let out for a few hours, because it's an emergency, see?'

'Oh, dear. Nothing wrong at home, is there? It's not your dad, is it?'

'Yes, and no. That is, yes, there is something wrong, but Dad's all right, so far as we know. It's Mam. She's in the cottage hospital, with a broken leg. She was up on a stepladder, in the shop, and she fell off.'

Ruth, busy making tea and wishing she had something to go with it, made all the right noises. 'Poor thing! I'll sit down and write a cheery note to her this evening.'

Ifor shuffled his feet. 'Well . . . er . . . Auntie Ruth, Mam was wondering if you could come and sort of take over while she's in hospital, like.'

'Oh, I don't think I could do that, love! I mean, there's your Uncle Bob, and the children; I have my hands full as it is.'

'But you don't work, Auntie,' he pointed out. 'And couldn't your Marina manage here while you're away?'

A spasm of annoyance welled up in Ruth. 'You don't work,' indeed! Just like a man! What would you call cooking and cleaning, washing and ironing and mending, not to mention queuing for food, and all having to be done after broken, fear-filled nights!

'Surely there's someone else who could help your mum? Someone nearer home?' she asked.

Ifor shook his head. 'Some of the neighbours are popping in, temporary like, but they all have their own families. And Mamgu can't do for herself, and of course there's the shop. The people registered there for rations can't do without it, see?'

Ruth did see.

She felt sorry for Dora, but it really

wasn't possible for Ruth to go running off to Wales. She had her own responsibilities. It wasn't as if Dora was Ruth's sister or anything. They were only cousins.

Ruth and Dora had spent a lot of time together as girls growing up in Gloucestershire, but then Ruth had married Bob and come to Hemel Hempstead, and Dora had wed a Welshman and gone to live with him in Carmarthenshire.

Over the years, their correspondence had dwindled until it had now reached the stage of little more than cards exchanged at Christmas and on birthdays.

'How long will your mother be in hospital?' she asked now. 'Did the doctors say?'

'It's a fractured femur,' Ifor told her, stumbling over the unfamiliar words. 'They've got her leg strung up with pulleys and she's to stay like that for about fourteen weeks. After that she has to have physiotherapy. Perhaps she'll never walk again,' he finished gloomily.

'Now, now, we'll have none of that defeatist talk here!'

'I can't help it, Auntie!' He brushed away a tear. 'Mam's so worried about Mamgu and the shop. I wish Dada was here, but he's away at sea, and since Idris went and joined the Navy, I just didn't know where to turn until Mam told me to come to you.'

Poor boy, Ruth thought.

Stalling for time, she refilled his cup and asked how he liked life in the Air Force. 'Training to be a pilot, are you?'

That raised a smile.

'Oh, no. I'm ground crew. We keep the planes in working order. It's good training, mind. After the war I'll be able to get a good job as a mechanic of some sort.'

That was one less thing for Dora to worry about. Most pilots were lads not much older than Ifor himself, but for many of them their life expectancy could be counted in weeks. With any luck, Ifor would be safe on the ground while still making a vital contribution towards the war effort.

'So, tell me what to do, Auntie,' he pleaded.

'You'll have to give me time to think, love. I'll have a word with your Uncle Bob when he gets in from work. Perhaps between the two of us we'll be able to come up with something, but I can't promise.'

'But how will I know what you've decided?' asked Ifor, looking even more worried than before.

'You leave me the phone number of your camp, and I'll ring up tonight from the phone box down the road. If they can't get hold of you, I suppose someone will take a message?'

He nodded, looking a little happier.

When he had gone, Ruth went back to her washing, her thoughts in a whirl. What on earth could she and Bob do to help? Dora might just have to close the shop. It would be an inconvenience for the customers who were registered there, but things like that were happening all

9

over Britain and people managed.

It was Mamgu who was the big problem.

Old Mair Thomas, Dora's mother-in-law, was more or less bedridden following a stroke she'd had just before the war. As Ruth knew from Dora's infrequent letters, she managed to care for the old lady with some occasional help from the district nurse, but it was obvious that Dora found looking after Mamgu a struggle. Fiercely independent, the old woman often tried to get out of bed on her own, and it was impossible to leave her unattended in case she had a fall.

'Oh, dear, but I can't go to Wales!' Ruth muttered, as she busied herself at the washboard. 'I can't be away from home for three months or more, and nobody could expect it of me.'

Dora would have to make her own arrangements, she thought, although it would have been lovely to get away for a while to a peaceful Welsh mining village. But she couldn't possibly leave the children. Who would see them safely out to the shelter on the nights when the sirens went and Bob was out fire-watching? And what if the worst happened and they were all killed while she was away looking after someone else's family? She would never forgive herself.

If only Marina was a few years older, then she could have been sent to Wales, but even if she could have coped with the old lady, there was still the shop to look after. There was a time when a capable youngster could have minded a small shop, but nowadays there was so much red tape involved, what with ration cards and quotas. Very likely the government had rules about who could be in charge. They probably had a minimum age.

No, sending Marina just wasn't possible, yet they must do something to help!

The kitchen was now full of steam, and a few damp tendrils of dark hair had escaped from under Ruth's turban.

She pushed them back, sighing. Life was full of problems.

But she would forget all about this one until Bob came home. Two heads were better than one. He might suggest that Dora should hire an assistant, some local woman who'd be glad of a few extra shillings in her purse. Why hadn't she suggested that to Ifor? Ah, well, she could bring that up when she phoned him, later.

* * *

'Oh, sorry! I was expecting to see Dr Stenson,' the man exclaimed as he stepped into the room.

The white-haired man seated behind the desk looked up with a sigh.

'Dr Stenson has joined up and I've been called out of retirement to take his place. I'm Dr Leacy. What can I do for you, Mr Greene?'

'It's this cough, doctor. I've got a tickle in my throat all the time and when I cough there's a pain in my chest. It's got me worried, I can tell you.'

'I'd better listen to your chest, then. Off with your jacket and shirt, please. Come along, man; I haven't got all day!'

Bob Greene did as he was told, reflecting that it was this older man who should have been sent to the army, not the amiable Dr Stenson. He would soon have put any malingerers in their place! But perhaps it was having to take over from Dr Stenson that had made Dr Leacy irritable; coming back into the practice when he'd been expecting to enjoy a leisurely retirement was no joke for a chap of his age.

'What is your occupation, Mr Greene?' The doctor had finished his tapping and thumpings and was now making a note on Bob's chart.

'I work at the bakery, Doctor. Making bread.'

'Hmm. Flour in the lungs, that's what's affecting you. I'm going to send you for an X-ray, just to make sure, but

I don't think there's any risk of tuberculosis. However, you'll have to give up working at the bakery.'

'But I can't stop work, Doctor! I've a wife and youngsters to support!'

'Who said anything about stopping? You'll just have to find another line of work, that's all. No chance of you going into the army, of course. It says here you had rheumatic fever as a boy and that's put the kibosh on that. Now, off you go, back to that bakery of yours, and be sure to give in your notice while you're about it. Doctor's orders, mind!'

Bob staggered out in a daze.

'And that's what the doctor told me, true as I'm standing here,' he told his employer half an hour later. 'I have to finish, no two ways about it.'

'Are you sure it's all that serious, Bob?' The baker frowned. 'I don't quite see the connection between flour getting in your lungs and this illness you had as a nipper. What does he say will happen to you if you keep on going the way you are?'

'I don't rightly know, Sid. I was so bamboozled I didn't think to ask. He just told me to give in my notice and chased me out of the surgery.'

'This is a right turn up for the books! Where am I going to get somebody reliable to replace you? All the good men have been called up! And people have to have bread, even if it is on ration and made of poor quality flour!'

'What about me?' Bob grumbled. 'I'm the only breadwinner in my family, if you'll pardon the pun! My Ruth is a good thrifty woman, but she can't manage on thin air.'

'Now, there's a thought,' Sid murmured. 'Would she like to take your place here? I could put Bessie on to bread and rolls, and your missus could do the cakes, such as they are. Not that she'd earn as much as you do, of course, being a woman.'

'No wife of mine is going out to work while I'm alive,' Bob snapped. 'I won't have it said that I can't provide for my family, and that's flat!'

'You're behind the times, man. Don't you know there's a war on? Lots of women are going out to work in factories and offices, taking the place of the poor devils who are away fighting for king and country. But it's up to you. If you say your Ruth can't come here, why, that's your business. I'll just have to look around for somebody else.'

★   ★   ★

Back at number 15 Jubilee Avenue, Ruth Greene was beginning to think about the evening meal. This being Monday, there was cold meat left over from Sunday and that, combined with home-grown salad, would make up the first course. But what could they have for pudding? Young Basil loved fried jam sandwiches but the batter would have to be made with the detested powdered egg, and his sister would turn up her nose at it, she knew.

Biting her lip, Ruth glanced out of the window, anxiously keeping an eye on the leaden sky. Her washing hung limply on the line, half dry. If it started to rain then she'd have to dash out to bring it all in and drape it over the clothes horse.

'Mum! I'm home! Is there anything to eat? I'm starving!' shouted Basil, coming in from school with his tie under one ear and his socks at half mast.

'You'll have to wait for tea, love. Your dad and Marina aren't home yet.'

Basil pulled a face that he fondly imagined characterised young love.

'Oh, her! She's standing down the end of the road ogling at a grammar school boy.' He made kissing sounds to illustrate his point.

'Now, that's enough of that, young Basil! I'm sure she's doing nothing of the sort.'

'Well, she's talking to him, anyway, and looking all goo-goo-eyed.'

'Your father will give her goo-goo eyes if he catches her.' Ruth laughed, pulling off her turban as she spoke.

17

'Out of my way, my lad. I must go and put my face on before your father gets home and sees me looking like this.'

Basil sauntered off, wondering if he could remove something from the bread bin without being caught in the act. What was the good of having a baker for a father if you couldn't get an extra crust now and then? The only pickings they ever got was stale bread that hadn't been sold. Good enough for toast, his mother said, and glad to get it.

It was only a few minutes later that Bob came home, but as soon as he came through the door, Ruth knew something was wrong. He looked so defeated. Was the war news bad? Was it something about the invasion?

'Bob! What on earth's the matter?'

'I had to see the doctor today,' he told her. 'Not Dr Stenson, he's been called up. It was an older chap; Leacy's his name.'

A dreadful fear gripped Ruth's heart. 'Are you all right, love? Oh, my goodness, come and sit down and I'll bring you a cup of tea.'

'No, no, just give me a minute, that's all.'

'Mum! Can I have my tea now that Dad's home?' called Basil.

'I couldn't eat a thing,' Bob groaned, putting his face in his hands. 'Give the boy my share.'

'I'll do no such thing. It's only a cold meal, being Monday. It can go back into the larder until you're ready for it. Meanwhile tell me what's bothering you.'

Moments later, Basil appeared at the sitting-room door, looking mutinous. 'Mum! I need my tea!'

'You'll get it in a minute, Basil. Now you can just go upstairs and get on with your homework.'

'But I told Frankie I'd . . . '

Suddenly Bob exploded. 'You do as your mother tells you, my lad, unless you want to feel the weight of my hand! And don't scruff along on your shoes like that. I'm not made of shoe leather!'

'But, Dad, I only . . . '

'Get out of my sight!' Bob roared, and Basil shot up the stairs without further ado.

Ruth felt her stomach clench. This wasn't like her Bob at all. He was quite strict with the children, especially with Marina — her being just a young girl — but it was rare to see him lose his temper. Something must have really upset him if he could fly off the handle like this.

'Tell me what's wrong,' she said softly.

'I've lost my job,' he told her, unable to meet her eyes.

'You've never had the sack!'

'No, of course I haven't, nothing like that; but it's worse in a way. I went to see the doctor about this cough of mine, and he says it's the flour getting in my lungs. He's made me give in my notice at the bakery because of it.'

A great sense of relief swept over Ruth. For a moment she felt quite faint. She didn't know what she'd been imagining, but nowadays you never knew what was likely to happen next, with that madman Hitler and his Nazis over in Germany.

'Oh, well, you'll soon find something else,' she soothed.

'Like what? They won't have me in the army because they say that rheumatic fever did something to my heart. I can't do heavy lifting for the same reason, so factory work is out. Now I'm told I can't follow my own trade, so what's left?'

Ruth smiled to herself as he continued to moan. Best to let him get it out of his system and then she'd spring her little surprise on him. It would kill two birds with one stone if they went to Wales. It would solve Bob's problem, and help Dora out at the same time. Really, this pronouncement of Dr Leacy's couldn't have come at a better time.

'I had a visitor today,' she said, smiling, when at last she could get a word in. 'You'll never guess who it was!

My cousin Dora's youngest, all grown up and in the RAF now, and stationed near here. It seems there's trouble at home. Dora's in hospital with a broken leg and there's nobody to look after things, not with her husband Dai and eldest lad Idris both being away at sea. That's where we come in!'

* * *

Bob listened to Ruth's story, then sat looking thoughtful. 'So you're suggesting we should all go down to Wales to help Dora's family?'

'Of course,' Ruth enthused. 'And you could work in the shop!'

'So could you.'

'Oh, I could give you a hand, but you'd be much better at dealing with all the ration books and suppliers and what-not. Besides, I'll be keeping house as usual, and looking after the old lady.'

'It's hardly likely to be a permanent job for me though, is it? Three or four months at the most, and then what?'

'We'll cross that bridge when we come to it, Bob! It'll fill a gap for now.'

'Hm, yes, but will your cousin be able to pay us anything?'

Ruth looked pained. 'She's family, Bob! You don't expect to get paid for helping out. Besides, we'll have no rent to pay, and I'm sure we'll be given our food there.'

'You don't understand what I'm getting at, pet. What about this house? If we expect to have it to come back to when this little expedition is over, then we'll have to keep shelling out the rent for it while we're gone. Where's the money to come from for that if I'm not earning?'

'Oh, I see what you mean. Well, let's give it up then. The landlord won't have any trouble letting it, not with so many people getting bombed out and made homeless all over the place.'

Annoyingly Bob continued to be the voice of reason. 'And what about all our furniture? Putting it in storage costs money too, you know. And my vegetable garden! I don't want to abandon that after all my hard work.'

Like many people, Bob had dug up his cherished lawn at the outbreak of the war, and was 'digging for victory' as the government slogan went. With most food items rationed, or missing altogether from the shops, it was vital for householders to produce as much food as they could.

'We've got to make up our minds soon,' Ruth reminded him. 'I promised to get in touch with Ifor this evening. As I see it, we've got two choices: either I take the children to Wales with me, leaving you to cope alone while you look for work, or we all go. Which is it to be?'

A plaintive voice came from the doorway. 'I've finished my homework, Mum, and I'm still hungry.'

'Basil!' Ruth bawled. 'Don't you know there's a war on?'

'I was only asking,' Basil muttered. 'No harm in that, is there?'

'It's all right, son,' Bob put in. 'Your mum and I are a bit busy at the moment, that's all. Have a look in my haversack. There are a couple of buns in there. Mind you give one to your sister.'

'Cor, thanks, Dad!'

'Blast this wretched war!' Bob said. 'There isn't even a bit of dried fruit in those buns. I feel sorry for kids today, I really do. Most of them have never even seen a banana or an orange, never mind tasted ice-cream.'

'If we worked at that grocery shop we'd have first pick of anything coming in,' Ruth said, with low cunning. 'I don't mean doing anything we shouldn't, of course; but so often supplies are limited and it's first come, first served. I can't tell you how many times I've stood in a queue waiting for something tasty, only to have them run out of whatever it is before my turn comes.'

'I've said it before, and I'll say it again; I won't have us separated,' Bob insisted. 'That's why I put my foot down over the kids being evacuated. If our number's up, then we'll all go together.'

'I know, dear,' Ruth spoke softly. 'I agree with you there. But why don't we all go to Wales? I haven't heard about them bombing so far inland, and it would be a relief to do without those air raids for a bit.'

Bob seemed to have arrived at a decision. 'I tell you what, old girl. I'll pop down the road and have a word with Pete Foster, our landlord. I'll make up my mind when I've heard what he has to say.'

★　★　★

When Bob returned he was grinning all over his face.

'Pete has an idea, love. I asked him about this house going for a short-term let, so that we could move back in later, and he said why not leave our bits and pieces behind? He could make more money letting it furnished as temporary accommodation for someone who's been bombed out, and it would save us putting all our furniture into storage.'

Ruth was doubtful at first, but she knew that nothing was ever certain while there was a war on. If a bomb fell on their home, they'd lose everything anyway.

'But I wouldn't want strangers getting hold of my good china,' she protested. 'That was a wedding present, that was! And what about our clothes? We can't take them all with us, and if they get stolen we won't be able to replace them for love nor money!'

'Pete thought of that, too,' Bob beamed. 'I'll put a padlock on the box room and all our personal stuff can go in there. Next objection, please!'

But Ruth had nothing more to say. She was all ready for the move. She'd even made a list of things to be done.

'I'd better get off and phone the camp where Ifor is stationed. Have you any change? I want to have plenty for the call box in case they keep me waiting while they fetch him. While I'm

27

gone you'd better discuss everything with the children. They'll have to be put in the picture.'

★　★　★

'You're sending us to Wales?' Marina stammered. 'I thought you said you wouldn't let us be evacuated? I want to stay here with you and Mum!'

'Me, too!' Basil piped up.

'You're not being evacuated. Well, not exactly. We'll all be going. You've heard your mother speak of her cousin in Wales, haven't you?'

'The one we call Auntie Dora?'

'Yes, that's right, Marina. Well, she's had to go into hospital, and that leaves nobody at home to look after either the shop or her mother-in-law. She's appealed to us for help. Your mother and I have talked it over, and we've agreed to give it a go. Luckily the school year is almost over, so there's no problem there.'

Basil had picked up his mother's list

and was studying it intently

'What's a mamgoo, Dad? Is it some sort of animal that we have to look after?'

'What? Let me see that.' Bob laughed. 'I think that's pronounced 'mamgee', son. It's the Welsh word for grandmother. She's Uncle Dai's mother, see?'

By the time Ruth returned, the children had accepted the idea of their temporary house move.

Marina didn't mind because her best friend was going to be spending the summer holidays with her grandparents in Torquay, leaving Marina at a loose end anyway. The idea of seeing new places and meeting new people was quite appealing. Since the war began, life had become quite boring — if you discounted the air raids!

Basil, poor boy, was entertaining greedy thoughts about all the food that would be available in a grocer's shop.

'How did it go?' Bob asked, when his wife finally returned. 'Did you get through? Did you manage to have a word with young Ifor?'

'Yes, to both questions. It seems that he was off duty and had spent the past hour hanging around the guard-house waiting for me to ring. I explained that it's going to be all of a week before we arrive, what with one thing and another. You have to work out your notice, and I must get busy with the packing.'

'I think I'll go out and take a look round the garden, love. I hope the new people, whoever they are, will take good care of my vegetables.'

Ruth laughed. 'They'll be only too glad to have the use of them.'

'Unless they're Londoners who think that everything grows on market stalls,' Bob retorted.

But Ruth knew that for Bob the fate of a few rows of brussels sprouts was the least of his worries. Only hours ago her husband had been holding down a regular job and now his world had changed in a flash.

All of a sudden she began to wonder if they were doing the right thing. Would she be able to deal with old Mrs Thomas? She hadn't any nursing experience, although surely bringing up children — with all the bathing and feeding and comforting that entailed — qualified her to look after one partially bedridden old lady. But how would Dora's mother-in-law feel about her home being invaded by a strange family? Ruth hoped she wouldn't be too querulous, especially since Basil was a normal little boy who tended to be noisy at times.

Oh, well, one thing at a time. They must look upon this as an adventure, and if things didn't work out, so what? It was only for a few weeks, after all.

A Long Journey

After an appalling journey which had involved changing trains several times, the Greenes finally arrived at their destination.

'How do we get in?' Ruth asked, of nobody in particular. The four of them were standing in the pouring rain outside Dora and Dai's double-fronted shop in the mining village of Bedwen, but there was no sign of life in the darkened grocer's.

'It's locked,' Bob announced, rattling the door handle to no avail. 'Surely someone must be expecting us. Perhaps the old girl is all alone in the house and can't get out of bed to let us in.'

'Round here, Dad!' Marina called, from somewhere in the gloom.

At the sound of her voice, the side door flew open, illuminating them all in a beam of light.

'Here you are at last! Don't stand out there in the damp or you'll catch your deaths!'

They crowded into a cheerful kitchen, dragging their bulging suitcases behind them, and were greeted by a small, plump woman with a cheerful expression.

'I'm Mrs Parry — Bessie, that is.'

'I'm Bob Greene, this is my wife, Ruth, and these are our children, Marina and Basil.'

Bob held out his hand to Mrs Parry and, having first wiped her hands on her apron, she accepted the handshake.

'Very pleased to meet you, I'm sure. Now, just pass me your wet things and I'll hang them up in the scullery. I've a nice rabbit pie keeping warm in the oven, and I'll have it on the table in two shakes.'

Basil gave a sudden whimper. His face was the colour of putty and his hair was plastered to his skull from the rain.

Mrs Parry looked at him with pity in her dark eyes.

'Poor little chap; he's all worn out. I'll just take him up and pop him into bed, and then I'll come down and see to your meal, all right?'

Ruth made a move towards the case containing Basil's pyjamas, but was waved aside by Mrs Parry.

'I'll see to him, Mrs Greene. You go through to the scullery and wash your hands and then come and sit by the fire. You can take him something on a tray later, if he's still awake, which by the look of him I very much doubt.'

Far from being annoyed at being told what to do, Ruth suddenly felt quite safe and secure in this cosy kitchen. It was pleasant to be taken care of instead of having to worry about getting the family settled in.

She was also glad to see that the strain had left Bob's face; he, too, seemed to relish handing over the reins of command for the time being.

'She's like one of those nannies that you read about in books where the children live in a nursery at the top of the house,' Marina whispered to her mother.

Ruth smiled. That described Mrs Parry exactly.

The kitchen was a large one, one wall taken up by a huge fireplace which obviously did double duty for cooking and heating. There was a hob on each side of the fire which burned brightly in the black grate, and an iron bar which could be swung over the flames was meant to hold a pot or kettle. A small black door in the fireplace wall opened into the oven where the pie was keeping hot.

The mantelpiece itself was covered with a variety of items, candlesticks, a pair of china dogs, and some photographs framed in passe-partout.

A huge Welsh dresser on the opposite wall was filled with blue and white crockery, while the remaining space held pots and pans suspended from big old iron nails.

There were rag rugs on the stone-flagged floor.

'What a lovely kitchen,' Ruth said sincerely, her tired eyes taking everything in. The room and its furnishings seemed timeless, and the war seemed very far away.

'There, he's all tucked up in bed.' Mrs Parry beamed at Ruth as she bustled back into the kitchen. 'I thought he wouldn't be long nodding off. Now, sit up to the table and get started on your meal.'

'Aren't you going to join us, Mrs Parry?'

'Na, na, Mr Greene. I had to go home to feed the family, see? I had mine then.'

Delicious though the food was, Marina soon began to droop.

'You'd better get off to bed as well, *bach*,' she was told by Mrs Parry. 'Up you go, now. You'll soon see where things are. There are three bedrooms and I've put you in Idris's old bed. The big room is Dora's and Dai's — you'll have that, Mr and Mrs Greene. I can't think where we'll put everyone when

Dora gets out of hospital, but there, we'll cross that bridge when we come to it. No need to worry about it tonight.'

'But where is Mrs Thomas, then?' Ruth was puzzled. There had been no mention of the old lady and obviously she wasn't sleeping upstairs.

'Oh, she's just next door.' Bessie Parry jerked a thumb towards the wall. 'That used to be the parlour, but when she came to live here after her stroke they thought it best to keep her downstairs. Makes less running up and down for poor Dora, you see? I've already looked in on her and she's all right. Dead to the world, she is. I'll introduce you when I come back in the morning. She wouldn't thank me for disturbing her now.'

'But what if she wakes up in the night? What do I do?' Ruth sounded worried.

'She keeps a bell at the side of the bed, but I doubt you'll hear from her. She's been sleeping badly ever since Dora had her accident — worrying, see — and the doctor prescribed tablets for her. The district nurse will drop in tomorrow and tell you all about her, but really, Mrs Thomas is doing quite well. It's just that she shouldn't be left alone in the house, especially at night when there's nobody to call on for help.'

'What about the shop, then?' Bob wondered. 'What time do we open up in the morning?'

'No need to worry about that, Mr Greene. I'll be back first thing to show you the ropes. Mind you, we've only been able to open it for two hours a day lately, what with one thing and the other, so people will be glad to see everything back to normal. Now, I must be off home or my man will think I've eloped with Jones the milk! We'll leave these crocks to soak in the sink till morning, all right?'

In a daze, Ruth watched the kindly little woman cram a felt hat on to her frizzy dark hair and shrug her arms into a shabby coat.

'I'll say *nos da*, then,' she nodded, as

she left by the side door.

Ruth had no idea what *nos da* was; probably a Welsh form of goodbye?

'Come on, love, it's been a long day.' Bob yawned. 'You go and check on the kids while I bring the bags up.'

Ruth went first to the little room where her son was sleeping. He was curled up on the bed, still wearing his vest and underpants, and the covers had slipped to the floor. Tenderly she put them back over him and tucked them round his shoulders, casting a quick look around the darkened room as she did so.

She felt a pang as she noticed the contents of the shelves; a few children's annuals, boxes containing games of ludo and snakes and ladders, and several pieces belonging to a toy train set. They were so obviously the cherished possessions of a boy not much older than young Basil, but now Ifor was far away from his childhood home, playing a man's part in this dreadful war. It was all wrong.

★ ★ ★

Lying beside Ruth in the strange bed, Bob was snoring softly. He had gone out like a light as soon as his head touched the pillow.

But Ruth, in that strange half-comatose state between waking and sleeping, found the events of the day flooding her mind.

She couldn't help thinking about the dreadful train journey they had endured from London to Cardiff which, she had been told, had taken twice as long as it would have done in peacetime. There had been so many lengthy and unex-plained stops that she'd often felt like screaming in frustration.

The train itself had been full to bursting, with passengers packed into the smoke-filled corridors. When, even-tually, an elderly man had got up and offered Ruth his seat, she'd sunk down gratefully, sure she would never be able to get up again.

Bob had commented on the various

uniforms that the other men on the train were wearing. Not only did these represent the army, navy and air force, but there were young men whose shoulder flashes proclaimed them to be from Canada or Australia.

Men and women seemed to have come from all corners of the empire to aid in the defence of the mother country and, with nothing else to do on their journey, these youngsters passed the time by singing — none too tunefully.

'Ten green bottles, hanging on the wall! If one green bottle should accidentally fall, there'd be nine green bottles, hanging on the wall!'

Basil joined in the singing with enthusiasm and, after listening with disdain for the first few verses, even Marina shook off her sulks and added her voice to the rest.

Ruth had felt a headache coming on. If only they could open a window! But she'd been afraid to get up in case somebody took her seat while she was on her feet!

But all that was behind them now. They had come to a safe haven and the adventure on which they were about to embark would provide them with a welcome break from the stress they had endured back in the Home Counties.

Turning over on to her side, Ruth slept.

Meeting Mair Thomas

'And here is Mrs Greene, come to stay with you!' Bessie Parry spoke brightly, like a jolly dentist assuring a squirming child that this wouldn't hurt.

The senior Mrs Thomas glared back, looking for all the world like an indignant owl. She was sitting bolt upright in an old-fashioned iron bed, clutching a crocheted shawl to her ample bosom. Incongruously she wore a battered felt hat pulled low over her eyes. This headpiece was decorated with what seemed to be an entire bird, minus a few feathers.

Ruth concluded that this peculiar garment was being worn either in honour of their meeting — just as no lady would dream of going out in public without her hat and gloves — or because Dora's mother-in-law was just downright odd.

'How do you do, Mrs Thomas?' Ruth murmured.

The old lady stared back at her without blinking.

Oh, dear! Couldn't she talk? Nobody had said that the stroke had robbed her of the power of speech. This was going to make things really difficult.

'Come on, *bach*, say something,' Bessie encouraged.

Mair Thomas responded with a flood of Welsh, accompanied by a series of violent nods.

'She's being a bit awkward this morning,' Bessie muttered in an aside to Ruth. 'Come now, Mrs Thomas, let's speak English. Mrs Greene has no Welsh, see?'

Frowning, the old lady looked Ruth up and down, her gaze taking in first the polished court shoes, then travelling over the shabby tweed skirt and hand-made cotton blouse. Her eyes half closed in horror as she studied Ruth's face.

Ruth felt as if she'd been weighed in

the balance and found wanting.

It's my lipstick! she decided. The old girl probably doesn't approve of makeup. Well, I'm blowed if I'm going to take it off, like a naughty schoolgirl. She'll just have to get used to it.

She cleared her throat. 'I'm glad we were able to come and help Dora in her hour of need,' she ventured, although surely, as the sole member of the family currently in residence, Mrs Thomas should have been the one making welcoming noises.

The old lady frowned again. Then, in a creaky voice, she asked, 'Are you Church or Chapel?'

'Er, we're Church of England, I suppose.'

A grim nod greeted this information. It was obvious that the older woman's worst fears had been realised.

'There now, isn't this nice?' chirruped Bessie Parry. 'The two of you are getting on so well together. You just sit here, Mrs Greene, and you can get to know each other while I go and give Mr

Greene a hand in the shop. There was a queue forming outside last time I looked, and he won't know where anything is, never mind how to work out what's what with the ration books.'

Left alone, the two women looked at each other warily.

Mair Thomas, still wearing her hat, slid lower under the quilt, reminding Ruth of a wary tortoise retreating into its shell when confronted by a curious cat.

Ruth, perched on the edge of her chair, was unsure what to do next.

She looked around her.

The room still bore evidence of its previous existence as a parlour. The window, with its worn burgundy velvet window-seat, looked out on to a busy side street, and the view no doubt furnished Mair Thomas with some amusement as people passed by outside. She must have friends in the community; perhaps some of them tapped on the glass and waved, or even stopped to chat when the window was open.

Ruth turned her attention to the two huge pictures on the wall, reproductions of Victorian paintings, in heavy, ornate frames. She'd seen similar ones before — 'When did you last see your father?' was the title of the picture showing a small cavalier boy, hands behind his back, facing a group of stern-faced puritans. The other painting showed Sir Francis Drake finishing his game of bowls at Plymouth Hoe before sailing off to defeat the Spanish Armada.

Ruth thought that she preferred these prints to the photograph of an elderly Queen Victoria which glowered down from Dora's bedroom wall. She decided that when she went up to make the beds she would turn the old girl's face to the wall.

Her reverie was interrupted by a tap on the door.

'Safe to come in, is it?' A uniformed nurse slipped into the room, beaming. 'I'm Nurse Jenkins. How do you do?'

'How do you do? I'm Ruth Greene.'

'What on earth are you doing in bed with your hat on, Mrs Thomas?' The nurse laughed as she dropped her bag on to the sideboard.

'It's a lovely day out there, now that the rain's stopped. As soon as you've had your blanket bath, we'll open that window and let you get some fresh air. Now then, I'm just going to have a word with Mrs Greene here, and then we'll get started.'

Glad to leave the over-warm room, Ruth followed the nurse out into the passage.

'Phew, that was uphill work,' she muttered.

'Oh, you'll soon get used to each other. She's come a long way since she had her stroke, but she's a bit resentful of the fact that she can't bustle about the way she used to. You can't blame her, can you?'

'I suppose not.'

'Moving in with her daughter-in-law was a big step for her, and poor Dora having to go away and leave her must have seemed like the last straw. She can get herself in and out of bed now, so she doesn't need a lot done for her any more, that's one good thing. You'll need to take her meals in on a tray, and deal with the commode, of course, but other than that the main thing is to have someone on the premises in case of anything unforeseen happening.'

'What sort of meals should I give her?'

'She's on a regular diet. She's a bit fussy, but you'll soon get used to that. Bessie Parry can give you some pointers, I expect. Basically, if the old girl throws her plate at you, you'll know that she doesn't like your cooking.'

Ruth's jaw dropped, and Nurse Jenkins threw her head back and roared.

'If you could see your face! Only joking, I was, see?'

'Very funny, I'm sure!' Ruth grunted.

★   ★   ★

Going through into the kitchen, Ruth found her daughter staring out of the window.

'It isn't like I'd imagined Wales to be, Mum.'

'What did you expect, people running round with harps tucked under their arms?'

'Oh, Mum! No, it's all these fields. You said this was a coal-mining place, and it doesn't look like that to me. And this is the only shop within miles, by the look of it. What on earth am I going to do here? I thought there would be a cinema at least!'

'We're on the outskirts here,' Bessie Parry explained, having heard Marina's words as she came in from the shop. 'We have the colliery, right enough, and before you go very far you'll see the coal tips, but this is sheep-farming country as well. And when you go down into the town you'll see plenty of other shops; we've got Broad Street and Quay Street and the High Street as well, full of shops they are.'

'Then why have this shop out here at all?'

'Because there are plenty of people living round about it. Why should they have to trudge two miles and back to the Home and Colonial, carrying a heavy shopping basket, when they don't have to?'

Catching sight of Marina's woebegone face she relented somewhat.

'But there, I don't suppose window shopping at the fishmonger's or the haberdashery is quite what you had in mind! But don't you worry, love, we have a very nice cinema, and there's quite a good library. We even have tennis courts and a football pitch down the Rec. I'll have to introduce you to my girl, Marged. She's about your age, and she can show you around.'

'You just have the one child, Mrs Parry? I was so exhausted when we came in last night that I can't quite remember what you said.'

Ruth was hoping for small boys, for Basil's sake.

'Oh, I have a son as well. Tim, that is. He's down the pit with his da. Nineteen he is, two years older than our Marged. But we'll soon find some friends for young Basil, never you fear. Over-run with little boys we are round here.'

Although feeling a little shy at the prospect of getting to know a strange girl, Marina looked forward to having someone to squire her around.

But when Mrs Parry eventually introduced her children with an air of motherly pride, it was Tim who impressed Marina the most. It took only one look to know that she was in love. With his dark eyes and black hair, the stocky young Welshman was quite the handsomest boy she had ever met.

'No, not a boy,' she corrected herself, 'a man.'

According to his mother he had been working at the colliery since leaving school at the age of fifteen, and bringing home a wage that was almost as good as that earned by his father. Marina felt sure that she had met her destiny. If only he would invite her to the pictures or something! Perhaps she should work on Marged to get him to ask her out.

* * *

On visiting day, Ruth went to see Dora in the cottage hospital. 'Thank goodness you've come!' Dora greeted her. 'I've been going mad wondering what's happening at home. Have you settled in all right? How are you getting along with Mamgu? Is there any word from the boys?'

'Whoa, one thing at a time!' Ruth laughed. 'Yes, we're beginning to get settled in, and here are a couple of letters which the postman handed to me just as I was leaving. And Mamgu is . . . well, Mamgu!'

'I know what you mean.' Dora sighed. 'I could put a different name to her, but Sister's got a swear box and I've contributed too much to it already, I'm afraid! Being strung up here is no joke, I can tell you!' She indicated the ropes and pulleys which kept her leg up in the air.

'It must be a real nuisance for you. But is Mrs Thomas really that difficult?'

'Well, of course I've tried to keep the peace, for Dai's sake. No man wants trouble between his wife and his mother, but the plain fact is she's never taken to me from the very beginning. She doesn't think I'm good enough for her precious son, even though I've been a good wife to him. But I'm not Welsh, and I'm not Chapel — although I do attend services at the Wesleyan Methodist and the boys have been brought up in that religion.'

'I think she believes I'm a scarlet woman because I wear lipstick,' Ruth said, grinning. 'I caught her giving me a really old-fashioned look. Actually, it reminded me of the look on Bob's face when Marina experimented with one of my old lipsticks and some rouge. He sent her upstairs quick sharp to scrub it off!'

'One of these letters is from Dai,' Dora gloated. 'I'll keep it to read later, for a treat.'

She fingered it lovingly before tucking it under her pillow.

'I wonder why Mrs Thomas dislikes the English so much?' Ruth mused. 'The whole town can't feel the way she does. Why, your friend Bessie Parry welcomed us with open arms.'

'I often think it's because Mamgu was born back in Victorian times, when things were very different here; no wireless and so on to introduce people to the outside world. As far as I know she's never been out of her own valley, so anyone from a bit farther afield is looked upon as outlandish and threatening. Folk have had the same outlook for centuries, I expect. It dates back to the days when strangers suddenly appearing meant trouble and had to be seen off.'

'But this is 1943, and there's a war on! We're all in it together, aren't we?'

'Yes, well, there are things you ought

to know about my mother-in-law, Ruth. She's had a hard life, one way or another. When she was still quite young there was a cave-in at the mine, and her two brothers were killed. Her father was on the same shift but they managed to get him out alive. He survived, but he was never the same again, and the family lived from hand to mouth from then on. It didn't help that the mine owners were English; not that that had anything to do with it, I suppose.'

'How dreadful!'

'It marked her for life, as far as I can see. Dai often heard his grandmother say that she didn't know how she'd have stayed sane after all that, if it hadn't been for her strong religious beliefs. Anyway, I understand that's why they let Dai go to sea. Mamgu said there was no way she was letting him spend his life underground, and that was that.'

'I can see why,' Ruth murmured, resolving as she spoke to try to be more patient with Mair Thomas if she could.

She looked around the ward, which at that moment seemed a cheerful place. The walls were lined with beds, twelve on each side of the long room, and there was a long cupboard in the middle, made colourful with numerous vases of flowers.

'The flowers are from our visitors,' Dora explained. 'Sister says it's better to have them there than on our bedside lockers, and that way everyone can share the enjoyment of them. Some people never get a visit at all. Either their homes are too far away, or they're all alone in the world. Still, there are worse places to be when you're feeling poorly. There's always something going on, something to see.'

'But you must get bored at times, trussed up like a Christmas turkey!'

'Oh, I can listen to the wireless when I want to,' Dora told her, indicating a set of headphones. 'And I have to admit that I'm getting a good rest here, being waited on hand and foot. The only thing I worry about is what would happen to me in an air raid, when I can't get out of this bed. Not that we've had any raids in this part of the world up to now, but if one did come, I'd be a sitting duck, never mind a turkey!'

Ruth felt it was time to change the subject.

'What do you think of the Parry children?' she asked Dora.

'Marged and Tim? Oh, they're nice enough, I suppose. Why do you ask?'

'Because Marina has started going about with the girl, ever since Bessie introduced them.'

'She'll come to no harm with Marged, Bessie will see to that.'

'I didn't think she would. It's just that Marina has her eye on Tim and I happen to know she's been pestering Marged to set up a date with him. Now they're all going to a sing-song at the Methodist chapel and Bob is less than pleased about it, I can tell you.'

Dora tried to hide a smile. 'Hardly a den of vice, is it? What's Bob afraid of?'

'I think he's afraid that Tim will ask

to walk Marina home, although between you and me, it's more likely to be the other way around! I've managed to persuade Bob to let her go if the girls promise to stay together as a group, but he's still not at all happy about it.'

'The girl is sixteen, Ruth! Almost a young woman. You can't keep her wrapped up in cotton wool for ever. Surely it's better to let her mix with boys in a controlled setting than wait until she's eighteen and called up into the women's services or something. Then she really will be like a lamb amongst wolves if she doesn't know how to look after herself.'

'And that's another thing!' Ruth sighed. 'According to Bob, there's a yawning gulf between Marina and Tim. She's just a schoolgirl and he's a grown man, for all there's only three years' difference in their ages.'

'Just stop worrying! It'll all come out in the wash!' Dora said blithely, with all the assurance of a mother of two boys.

Irritation flooded through Ruth.

Bringing up a daughter was no joke, and she and Bob were just beginning to find that out!

* * *

Unbeknown to Ruth, Bessie Parry was at that very moment having a quiet word with her son on the subject of Miss Marina Greene.

'Sweet on you, she is, *cariad*.'

'Never!'

'There's none so blind as those who won't see, son.'

'That's silly, Mam. It's just a schoolgirl crush, if anything. Besides, I'm thinking of asking Catrin Harris to walk out with me.'

Bessie's eyes brightened. 'Well, now, that would be very suitable, I'm sure!'

'Don't go planning the wedding just yet, Mam!' Tim chuckled. 'I'm just taking the girl to the pictures, that's all.'

But Bessie went about her work with a spring in her step. One of these days, Tim would be ready to settle down, and when he was, Catrin Harris was just the sort of girl she would have chosen for him. A local girl, and a miner's daughter, Catrin would know exactly what was expected of her as a miner's wife.

Meanwhile, it looked as though Marina might be making a nuisance of herself, always hanging around, coming to the house with some excuse — such as wanting to borrow a book from Marged — but really on the off-chance of running into Tim.

Marged, of course, lost no time in teasing her brother about being a heart-throb. While his fond mother believed that Tim was by far the best looking young man for miles around, to Marged he was just the brother she'd grown up with. He was all right, she supposed, but nothing to write home about!

'That girl can make eyes at him all she likes,' Bessie told Marged, 'but it won't do her any good, see. Now, what I want you to do, Marged Parry, is to introduce her to some of the grammar school boys, some nice lads her own age. Once she gets to know some of them, she'll leave our Tim alone. Emlyn Richards, now. She could get to fancy him.'

'Yes, Mam.' Marged answered her mother meekly, but she had no intention of letting Marina get anywhere near Emlyn. She wanted him for herself! They might make up a foursome, though, if Emlyn could find someone who was halfway decent for Marina.

'And don't forget you promised to do something about young Basil,' Bessie continued. 'He can't spend all his time kicking an old tin can along the street the way he was doing yesterday. Don't some of your friends have little brothers that he can play with?'

'Yes, Mam.' Marged went upstairs to tidy her room before Bessie could get started on that subject.

*   *   *

Feeling bored, Basil had eventually taken himself off to the recreation ground, known locally as 'the Rec'. Other than some rundown tennis courts and some goalposts, the place didn't have much to recommend it, but it did provide somewhere for children to let off steam.

Standing on the sidelines, Basil watched enviously as a group of boys kicked a soccer ball about to the accompaniment of shouts and laughter.

When the ball suddenly came his way, he didn't hesitate for a moment. Instead of simply kicking it back into play, he sprang into action, dribbling the ball until he reached the middle of the throng.

If there was one thing he was good at, it was playing football. The boys watched him appreciatively, and when one of the largest called out, 'Want a game?' he joined in eagerly.

By the time the other boys had drifted off to their homes, he was one of their number and had agreed to join their side the next day, when they were to play against another team in a friendly match.

'What on earth have you done to your sandals?' his mother snapped when at last he reached home, hot and dishevelled.

'Nothing, Mum.'

'Nothing! I'll give you nothing, my boy! Just look at those toes, all scuffed. If they get worn out you'll have to keep wearing them, holes or no! Even if we could afford a new pair for you, I don't know where we could find them. There's nothing in the shops. Don't you know there's a war on?'

Basil let his mother's tirade flow over his head. What a fuss about nothing! Wisely he didn't mention that he'd been playing football. He knew that he wasn't supposed to kick a ball about while wearing his sandals, but what else could he have done? Did she expect him to race all the way home to get into his boots, and then turn right around to go back to the recreation ground? By that time, the other boys would have gone their separate ways and Basil would have lost his chance. As it was, he'd been accepted by them, and he'd be going back again tomorrow.

'Sorry, Mum!' he said cheerfully, before she had the chance to tell him that he had to stay in as a punishment.

'All right, but don't let it happen again!' she scolded.

★   ★   ★

The next day, Ruth caught Basil as he was slinking out of the house, hoping to be unobserved by anyone, especially his mother.

'And where do you think you're going, Basil Greene?' she called out.

'Up the Rec. Some boys have asked me to play on their team. I've got my boots on, like you wanted.'

Ruth nodded, glad to know that he was making friends. Mind you, if she'd known what this football match would lead to, she wouldn't have been so complacent, but she had too much on her mind to worry about unforeseen consequences.

Bob, too, was fitting into his new surroundings. In fact, it was a long time since she'd seen him so relaxed and cheerful.

'Len Parry's invited me to drop in at the Red Dragon on Saturday night,' he told her. 'Len says he'll introduce me to some of the local chaps. You don't mind, do you, love? I wish you could come, but women don't go into pubs around these parts.'

'That's all right, love. You go and have a nice time. Perhaps I'll invite Bessie over for a cuppa. The young people are going to a debate at the chapel, and she'll be all on her own.'

The Red Dragon was crowded, and Bob listened with interest to what the miners had to say — spoken in English, so he wouldn't feel left out.

Most of them seemed well educated, or at least well-read, and the conversation was lively. It was easy to see why

Wales had the reputation of being a nation of orators.

'It's good of you to come here to run the shop for poor Dora,' one burly man said. 'How could you get away from your job in England? On your holidays, are you?'

'Not exactly. I'm out of work at the moment.'

'What trade you in, then?'

'I'm a baker, but I've had to pack it in — doctor's orders. Lung trouble, caused by all the flour, so he says.'

'Ah! Something like the silicosis miners get.' His new friend nodded. 'Coal dust, see?'

'They won't even take me in the army,' Bob went on. 'A dicky heart caused by rheumatic fever as a lad, or so I'm told.' He always felt compelled to explain why he wasn't serving in the armed forces. People were inclined to look down their noses at you if you weren't in uniform. They didn't go so far as to bestow a white feather on you, like they used to do in the Great War, but he still didn't want people to think he was a slacker.

Next the talk turned to the rumours about German spies being parachuted into Britain. Bob had heard them all before when he was in the Home Guard. If you noticed anything suspicious at all, you were supposed to perform a citizen's arrest and ask questions later.

'I expect the same thing is happening on our side,' he offered to the discussion. 'Our lot being dropped into occupied territory, I mean. Perhaps to link up with the Resistance. How else are we supposed to know what's going on?'

The evening passed so quickly that he was quite surprised when the landlord called for last orders. Apparently closing time was eleven o'clock, and the local bobbies were strict about enforcing the law.

'Of course, the pubs don't open tomorrow,' Len reminded him. 'Sunday, see. No drinking in Wales on the Sabbath.'

Another custom that Bob found unusual was that every man got to his feet for the singing of the Welsh national anthem before leaving the building. Bob had never seen anything like that in England, not that he had been much of a pub goer as a rule.

'Here you are, then.' Bessie smiled at him when he arrived back at what he was beginning to think of as home. She stood up, rolled her knitting into a neat bundle and stowed it in a clean flour bag. 'I hope my Len took good care of you, Mr Greene.'

'Yes, thank you. Very kind. Would you like me to see you home?'

'Na, na. It's only a few steps, and I don't suppose Hitler will be hiding round the corner to make a grab for me. If he is, I'll poke him in the eye with my knitting pins!'

Laughing, she made for the door, fastening her cardigan as she left.

'Is Marina in yet?' Bob asked Ruth, looking up at the ceiling as he spoke.

'Bless you, yes! It's gone eleven!

She's been in bed this past hour, and Basil's been up there since nine o'clock, reading his *Beano*. And Mrs Thomas is all tucked up, too, so it's just you and me. Do you fancy a nice cup of Horlicks?'

'Not on top of two pints of ale, thanks. I wouldn't mind something to eat, though. Have we got anything spare?'

'I could do you some bubble and squeak,' Ruth offered. 'It's a good thing we have Dora's garden to rely on. At least we won't go short of vegetables while we're here.'

Upstairs, their son was lying on his back on top of the covers, deep in thought. His football game had gone well, and he'd managed to score two goals which had made him popular with the other boys.

When the game had been over, they'd invited him to go down to the river with them, where they'd lain on their stomachs, trailing their hands in the water in the vain hope of catching a

70

fish. As with their elders, the boys' talk of the moment had to do with the possibility of spies in their midst, and what they would do if one was sighted. They boasted that they would bring the spy down with a rugger scrum, and sit on him while they tied him up using knots which some of the older boys had learned in the Scouts.

'But what if he's got a gun?' Basil asked. 'We might get shot.'

There was silence for a long moment as they considered this.

Then Rhodri, the oldest boy, who by common consensus was the leader of the gang, frowned at Basil. 'Where d'you get your name from, then? Funny sort of name, it seems to me.'

'It's not in the Bible,' another lad chimed in.

'How would you know?' Basil scoffed. 'I bet you haven't read the Bible. Not *all* of it, anyway.'

'Everybody knows that Basil isn't in the Bible, and it's not a Welsh name, either.'

'That's because I'm not Welsh!' Basil was no cissy and he could stick up for himself. 'Where I come from, they've never heard of some of your names either. Gwilym and Dewi and Meurig. I bet those aren't in the Bible either, so there!'

There was a low growl from the group of boys, and for a moment Basil thought he was going to have to run for it.

Rhodri stepped up and thrust his face into Basil's. 'Where you from, then, eh?'

'Hemel,' Basil replied. 'We're from Hemel.'

They left him alone then, and he was free to wander home without hindrance. So why was it that he had a sick feeling in his stomach and felt that he hadn't heard the last of this?

A Wonderful Day For Mamgu!

Ruth was still struggling to get along with Mamgu. It had reached the point where she had to steel herself to go into the older woman's room, which irritated Ruth no end. It wasn't as if Mair Thomas was openly rude or difficult; it was the silent treatment that was hard to take.

Ruth took in tasty meals on a tray to her, only to have her good food looked at glumly.

'Anyone would think I was giving her bread and scrape,' she complained to Bob. 'It's not my fault if there isn't much variety — that's down to rationing; she gets the same as us, and plenty of it. Honestly, it bothers me to see her pushing good food around her plate as if I'm a rotten cook!'

'Ah, but she polishes her plate clean, doesn't she? I haven't noticed a crumb coming back to the kitchen, for all she's so old and feeble.'

'Still . . . ' Ruth grumbled.

Nurse Jenkins came in only once a week, so it was left to Ruth to perform what she thought of as nursing tasks, which included washing Mamgu's face and hands, combing her long white hair, and making the bed. Ruth also cleaned the room every day, unhappily aware of Mamgu's beady eyes on her as she trundled the carpet sweeper over the faded rug.

'She makes me feel like an unsatisfactory housemaid,' Ruth moaned to Marina. 'She doesn't take her eyes off me for a minute. Perhaps she thinks I'm going to run off with the family valuables, such as they are.'

'Oh, Mum! Don't exaggerate!'

'Exaggerate my foot! You try looking after her and see how she treats you!'

'No fear! It's not my job, is it? I didn't ask to come down here to the back of beyond where there's nothing to do and nowhere to go!'

Caught between the devil and the deep blue sea, Ruth decided to take a break and to go to visit Dora at the cottage hospital.

'Come for me to cheer you up, have you?' Dora grinned.

'What do you mean?'

'Well, you've got a face like a wet weekend, old girl. Mamgu playing you up, is she?'

'Not really; she's just giving me the silent treatment. I must admit, though, it's getting me down a bit.'

Ruth had decided not to say too much about Mair Thomas. True, Dora had had a private moan about life with her mother-in-law, but she might get defensive if an outsider went on in the same vein.

'No, it's Marina who's playing me up. I don't know what's come over that girl. She used to be such a sweet little thing, and now she's as grumpy as a bear. She snaps back at everything I say, and as for helping me around the house, why, wild horses couldn't drag her anywhere near the washing up.'

'Get Bob to have a word with her, why don't you?'

'Bob? A fat lot of good that would be! She's all sweetness and light when he's around, so he doesn't see the awkward side of her.'

' "Sweet sixteen and never been kissed",' Dora quoted. 'I bet that's what's wrong with her, Ruth. Didn't you tell me she has her eye on that young Parry chap?'

'Oh, him! I was a bit worried for a while, but it seems to have come to nothing, and I must say, I'm glad. He's nice enough but he's too old for her. Three years' difference is nothing when you get to our age, but she's a sixteen-year-old schoolgirl and he's a working man, going on for twenty.'

'You've said all this before, and my advice was to let things run their course. You know what they say about forbidden fruit tasting the sweetest?

How do you know they're not seeing each other on the sly?'

'Because Bessie told me that he's courting a girl his own age called Catrin Harris. Very suitable, according to his mother. I think she has hopes that it'll come to something, and why not? With the wage he's bringing in he could probably afford to get married in a couple of years, and what's more, being in a reserved occupation he won't get called up. Of course, this explains why Marina's been going around with a face like a thunderclap. She knows there's no chance for her.'

'She'll have to worship from afar, then, won't she? Never mind, she'll change her tune when some other likely lad comes on the scene. What about my Ifor?'

'What about him?'

'I daresay he'll be coming home on leave one of these days. Perhaps they'll take a shine to each other?'

'But they're cousins.'

'Only second cousins.'

Ruth murmured something noncommittal. She couldn't say so to Dora, of course, but privately, she regarded Ifor as a bit wet behind the ears. She couldn't imagine how he was getting on in a barracks full of older and tougher men. She hoped that the timid lad wasn't getting bullied. Marina would make mincemeat of him, she was sure.

'How's Bob getting along in the shop?' Dora asked. 'I want to be able to tell Dai all about it when I write. There isn't much I can tell him about life in the hospital — one day here is much the same as the next, and anyway, the last thing he needs is to read about my moans, especially when there's nothing he can do about it.'

'How is Dai?'

'Safe and well, as far as I can make out. Of course, he can't say where his ship goes or what he's doing, because everything is censored, so his letters are a bit dull, too. But at least when I get one then I know he's still alive. Or, at least, he was when he sat down to write it.'

An uncomfortable few minutes passed as they contemplated this, until Ruth felt compelled to break the silence.

'Bob loves it in the shop. With his smiles and banter, he's got all the local ladies eating out of his hand. He seems to love meeting the public. There was nothing like that at the bakery, of course; it was all working behind the scenes there.'

There was a sudden clatter which drew all eyes to the end of the ward, where a hapless probationer had managed to let a tray slip through her fingers.

'Now the fat's in the fire!' Dora grinned. 'Just keep your eye on Sister and you'll see why they call her Captain Bligh!'

Sure enough, Sister had sailed down the ward and was now castigating the drooping nurse. Sister kept her voice low, but they could tell that she was bristling with indignation, and after a few minutes the girl picked up the bits and pieces and fled through a nearby door.

'That's the sluice,' Dora explained, 'the place where they wash bedpans and all that. It's also the place where they hide from Sister when they want an illicit smoke or — more often — a little weep.'

'Poor girl,' Ruth sympathised. 'Accidents happen, so why be so hard on her? I wonder what Sister said?'

'Oh, I can tell you that, I've heard it often enough — 'You'll never make a nurse, Nurse!' '

They laughed at the absurdity of it, and then Ruth consulted her watch.

'If I run I might just catch the four o'clock bus. If I miss it, I'll have an hour to wait and it looks like it's about to rain.'

They kissed the air above each other's cheeks, and Ruth hurried away, pausing at the door to wave back at Dora.

The outing had done Ruth good, and

she was full of high spirits as she went to catch her bus.

*   *   *

When Ruth reached home the shop was closed, as it usually was at that time of day. The locals knew that they could always tap on the side door if they needed something after hours, although most women preferred to shop as early as possible so as not to miss a share of some coveted item that had been delivered that morning.

Ruth hoped that Bob had kept the fire on in the kitchen, where the kettle was kept perpetually steaming on the hob.

But Bob was nowhere to be found. Was he in the garden, hoeing the vegetables?

Ruth peered out of the window, but the yard was deserted.

Then she heard the murmur of voices coming from Mamgu's room. It wasn't the day for Nurse Jenkins to call; was

Bessie in there, trying to cheer the old lady up?

Ruth tapped on the door and went in.

What she saw made her jaw drop with amazement. There was Bob, in his shirt sleeves and with his tie off, sprawled in a chair, babbling on about some funny incident that had taken place back when he'd worked in the bakery, while Mamgu was listening with rapt attention.

As Ruth watched, the story came to an end, and Mamgu responded with an open-mouthed grin, showing her false teeth.

What was going on here? Not only had Bob come into the holy of holies and sat himself down, but Mamgu was actually smiling!

'What on earth were you doing in Mamgu's room?' Ruth wanted to know once she had a moment to ask Bob about it. Not that she minded, of course, but she was surprised by it.

Bob shrugged. 'I don't know. I had

nothing better to do, and I felt sorry for the old girl, I suppose, sitting in there all alone with nobody to talk to. She must get lonely.'

Ruth had already taken Mamgu's tray in to her, and the rest of them were sitting around the kitchen fire, having their own meal.

'Vegetable pie again?' Basil grumbled. 'Where's the meat?'

'Eat what you've been given and be thankful,' his mother said automatically. 'If you don't like it, write and tell Herr Hitler.'

'I was thinking,' Bob went on, 'that there's really no reason why Mrs Thomas has to stay in that room, not now that she seems to be getting better. She should be in here with us. The only trouble is, she can't hobble more than a few steps, so how could we manage to get her in here?'

'There's a wheelbarrow out the back, Dad. Mamgu could use that,' Basil piped up, smirking.

'That will be quite enough, young

man! No, I shall make enquiries to see if anyone knows of a wheelchair we could borrow. Just think, Marina could take the old girl down town. The fresh air would do them both good.'

Marina's face showed just what she thought of that idea!

Ruth wasn't sure whether Bob was serious or not; he was good at joking with a straight face. But whatever the truth of the matter, it appeared that Bob was genuinely interested in Mamgu's well-being, because he soon came up with another idea.

★   ★   ★

'I've been looking at that reclining chair in Mamgu's room,' Bob announced the following morning.

'Yes, I rather fancied that myself,' his wife told him. The chair was made of highly polished wood and upholstered in a plum coloured uncut moquette. It looked fairly old, but Ruth had decided to look out for something similar once they were back home. She might find one like it in a second-hand shop.

'Next time you're in Mamgu's room, have a look at the back of it, Ruth. It goes up and down like a deckchair. A piece of the frame folds out and can be pushed into one of three slots so you can choose to sit up fairly straight, or lean back in one of two positions. Well, if you have no objection, I'm going to bring that chair in here for Mrs Thomas. It may take a while for her to shuffle across the floor to get in here, but with one of us on each side, she should be able to manage it.'

'Well, of course I don't object, love! It would be too bad if I did, when she's in her own home and we're the visitors. I don't know what she'll say to the idea, though. You know how shy she is.'

'You just leave her to me, love. I have my winning ways, you know.'

Ruth was amazed when Bob explained his plan to Mamgu and she saw the yearning look which came into the old lady's eyes. Ruth was quite sure that if she'd been the one to mention it, she'd have met with a firm refusal, or been subjected to the silent treatment again.

*   *   *

When old Mrs Thomas was comfortably installed in the kitchen, wiping a tear from her eye at the pleasure of it all, Ruth had to admit that Bob had handled the situation very nicely.

Bessie Parry, calling in to see if all was well, clapped her hands in glee when she saw what had taken place.

'There's lovely to see you sitting out, Mair, *bach*!' She smiled. 'The kitchen today, the shop tomorrow, isn't it?'

A flood of Welsh erupted from Mamgu. Although Ruth couldn't understand a word of it, she could tell from the old lady's face that she was delighted by this turn of events. This would certainly be something for Ruth to tell Dora on her next visit to the hospital.

Yet again Ruth felt sorry for the

impatience she so often felt when dealing with Mair Thomas. No wonder the poor dear was grumpy when she had nothing to do, hour after hour, but reflect on her woes. Her only son was away at sea, facing goodness knew what dangers, and her grandsons, too, were in the thick of things, and what could Mamgu do to help? Nothing at all, being forced to sit in bed all the time like a bump on a log.

Bessie Parry turned to Marina and handed her a note. 'This is from our Marged, *bach*. Make sure she gets it, she told me, as if I could forget!'

The envelope was a brilliant mauve, and smelled of violets.

'Thanks, Mrs Parry. I'll read it later.'

The girl rushed from the room and Ruth hid a smile.

'Later, my foot! She can't wait to see what it's about, and she doesn't want us to see her face while she's reading it!'

Ruth could recall her own teenage years, and now found it rather sweet to watch the girls with their little secrets.

Marged lived just a few yards down the road and could easily have popped in with her news, whatever it was. But no, sending a dramatic little note was much more interesting. It probably ended with 'don't tell a soul' or 'eat this'!

★　★　★

Marina found the note entirely satisfactory. Marged had managed to persuade Tim to go with them on a picnic 'up the mountain' and Emlyn Richards would be going with them to make up the numbers.

Marged warned Marina not to say a word to anybody about the two boys going with them, in case Mr and Mrs Greene put a stop to it.

Talking Tim into going along with the plan had taken some doing.

'Picnics, is it? I'm a grown man, Marged. I've better things to do with my time than go hiking up the mountain with a sandwich in my pocket!'

'You'd go like a shot if Catrin Harris was invited!'

'That's different.'

'Please, Tim! Marina wants to see Emlyn Richards, only her father won't let her go unchaperoned. He says she's too young for boyfriends. But if we went too, then he'd think there was no harm in it.'

Tim looked at her through narrowed eyes. 'I thought *you* were sweet on Emlyn Richards?'

'That was just a passing fancy,' Marged lied. 'Marina can have him, and welcome.'

'Well, I'll see if Catrin wants to come. I might be interested then.'

That wasn't what Marged had in mind, but there was nothing she could do about it. Anyway, it might turn out to be the best thing in the long run if Marina had to watch Tim spooning with Catrin. She'd know then that there was no hope for her. It was being cruel to be kind, as Mam would say.

However, as it turned out, Catrin

turned up her nose at the idea. 'I said I'd go to the pictures with Gwyneth on Saturday, Tim.'

'Can't you do that another time?'

'No, I can't. It's 'For Me And My Gal' and I've been waiting to see that.'

'Then I'll take you myself one evening. It's going to be on all week.'

'No, I don't want to let Gwyn down, not now we've made all our arrangements. Anyway, what's so special about going up that old mountain? We've been going up there all our lives. If it's having a meal with me you're after, you can come to the house and have your tea at the table. There's silly you are, Tim Parry!'

Somehow this caught him on the raw. 'There's nothing silly about wanting to spend time with the girl you love,' he said huffily.

'Don't be such a baby! Just because I want to go out with Gwyneth for once, it's not the end of the world. We can go up the mountain any old time.'

'Well, if that's how you feel!' Tim was

red in the face now, and beginning to feel sorry for himself.

Catrin's eyes flashed. 'I won't be bossed around by the likes of you, Tim Parry! You don't own me, and if I want to go out with Gwyneth, then I will. So put that in your pipe and smoke it!'

Catrin turned away and marched down the street with as much dignity as she could muster while tottering on high-heeled sandals.

Tim stared after her, seething. Well, he'd show Miss Harris a thing or two! He'd go along on this picnic and make sure that Catrin got to hear about it. He wouldn't let on that it was being arranged so that young Emlyn could get to know the visitor from England. Let Catrin think he was interested in the girl himself.

Marged was delighted when she heard about it. 'Mind you don't tell Mam that Emlyn is coming with us,' she warned Tim.

'Why not? Mam likes him, doesn't she?'

'I know that, but she might let it slip to Mrs Greene.'

Tim shrugged. None of that was his business.

That was when his sister had raced upstairs to write a jubilant note to Marina.

All she had to do now was make Emlyn Richards fall in with their plans, and that shouldn't be difficult because he'd been dropping hints about fancying Marina. And when he saw that Marina was only interested in Tim, then he would turn to Marged!

Spies!

Ruth leaned out of the window, frowning. Basil was at it again, aimlessly kicking a tin can down the street.

'What on earth is the matter with that boy, Bob? He looks like he's lost a shilling and found sixpence!'

Her husband frowned. 'He's not getting into mischief, is he?'

'Well, no, but at this rate it won't be long before he does. Basil! Coo-ee!'

Summoned by his mother, Basil trudged reluctantly back to the house.

'Don't you have anything better to do, child?' she questioned him.

He shook his head.

'Then why not go up to the recreation ground and see if there's a game of football going on? Won't the other boys be there at this time of day?'

'I dunno.'

Ruth lost patience with him. 'Either

you go and find out or you can put in an hour weeding the garden. Now, which is it to be? I don't want the neighbours to see you moping around like a wet weekend. They'll think I'm not bringing you up properly.'

'All right, Mum.' Basil wandered off, his head hanging low.

'And pick up your feet!' Ruth bawled after him. 'Or you'll have the soles worn through. Do you hear me?'

Basil headed for the recreation ground but, surprisingly for that time of day in the summer holidays, it was completely deserted.

He supposed he'd better go and see if his erstwhile friends were down by the river. Mum would be sure to ask if he'd met them, and he knew better than to fib.

The other boys stared at him without speaking as he approached. He was uncomfortably reminded of that picture in Mamgu's room, with the cross-looking men questioning the cavalier boy. Dad had explained to him about a civil war that had happened in the olden days, which meant that the English had been fighting each other instead of being pitched against an enemy, like now. The bad men wanted to catch the boy's father and they were trying to make him tell. The picture had impressed Basil. He would never betray his own father, no matter what anyone tried to do to him.

Rhodri Evans was the first of the boys to speak.

'Hey, you! When we asked you where you come from you said Hemel, didn't you?'

'Yes. So what?'

'So I told my da and he says that's the German word for heaven, see?'

Basil's jaw dropped. 'I never knew that. Names aren't supposed to mean anything. They're just places.'

'Da says we all come from heaven in the beginning. So now we know what you are, Basil Greene. You're a spy!'

It was a moment before Basil managed to find his voice.

'Don't talk daft! I'm nine years old! They wouldn't drop me out of an aeroplane on a parachute. I've never been up in a plane in my life.'

'Ah, but you're only camo-whatsit, that's what I think.'

'Camouflage,' another boy supplied.

'That's it. Your da is the real spy, see.'

Basil's first impulse was to leap forward and bop the older boy on the nose, but something told him that it would be better to keep quiet and hear what else was said. Being accused of spying was a serious business. You could go to prison, or worse.

'My father is not a spy. He works in a grocer's shop.'

But Rhodri kept on, confident that he knew what he was talking about.

'My father told me what he read in the paper,' he said, loudly and confidently. 'Not all spies get sent here by parachute. There are others who pretend to be ordinary people. They've been living here since before the war, and they change their names so that we think they're English, and then they try to find out things to tell the enemy. I bet that's what your da is up to!'

'My father's English!' Basil shouted. 'And he'd never do anything like that!'

'So you say. So why did he just turn up here in the middle of the war, when he should be fighting in the army or something? It looks fishy to me.'

'He wanted to be in the army, but they wouldn't let him join. I think he's too old or something. And we came here to help Auntie Dora, 'cos she's in hospital, and Uncle Dai is away at sea. Somebody has to look after the shop and the old granny.'

Blank stares greeted this explanation.

'I bet he's got one of those radios hidden away so he can send messages to Hitler,' Rhodri persisted.

It was useless to keep protesting, Basil knew. Their minds were made up and nothing he could say would make any difference.

'You're all nuts!' he shouted. 'And I'm not staying here to listen to this.

I'm going home!'

'Good riddance to bad rubbish! And you tell your da that we're on to him!'

Basil ran until his chest hurt and he had to stop. He was gripped by a dreadful fear. Of course his father wasn't a spy! Any fool would know that! But the whole country seemed to be gripped by spy fever. Even the posters at the railway station, with their frightening slogans, seemed to indicate that you had to be on your guard all the time. *'Careless talk costs lives.' 'Be like Dad, keep Mum.' 'Loose lips sink ships.'*

Should he warn Dad about what the boys had said about him? He knew from half-overheard conversations between his parents that people accused of being enemy aliens were being taken from their homes and locked up in prison camps.

Basil didn't know what an alien was, but it sounded sinister.

Could that happen to them?

The trouble was, if he went home

and said anything, his parents would simply laugh and tell him not to be so silly — that the boys were talking through their hats, as the saying went. Perhaps it was best to keep quiet for the moment. The boys might not do anything, and if they did speak out, nobody paid attention to children anyway.

*   *   *

'I'm worried about Basil,' Ruth told her husband some days later. 'Do you think he's sickening for something? He looks like he's seen a ghost, and yesterday tea-time he even refused pudding. That's not like him.'

'He's just bored, love. Missing his old friends, I expect. What happened to those lads he was playing football with?'

'He doesn't seem interested in them any more. I expect they've fallen out, the way kids do.'

Bob told her not to worry. It was bound to sort itself out in time. But

Ruth did worry. Wasn't that what mothers were for?

When she went up to tuck her son into bed that night, she sat down beside him to have a little chat.

'Everything all right, is it, love?'

'When are we going home, Mum? I don't like it here.'

'Missing your friends, are you? I'm afraid we can't go back just yet. You know why we're here. We have to wait until Auntie Dora is on her feet again and everything gets back to normal.'

'How long is she going to be in hospital, Mum?'

'Quite a while yet, I'm afraid. And then she has to have physiotherapy — that means exercises to strengthen her muscles. When people lie in bed for a long time, their muscles get flabby.'

'Then how am I going to get to school when September comes?'

'That's something your dad and I will have to discuss when we get a minute. I expect we'll have to see about putting you in the school here. You'll fall behind if we don't.'

Basil was horrified. If he was forced to attend school five days a week, then he'd be at the mercy of those boys and others like them.

'Can't I go to boarding-school?' he bleated.

'Boarding-school? Whatever gave you that idea? Of course you can't! We've hardly got two halfpennies to rub together, let alone hundreds of pounds to send you away. Now you roll over and go to sleep. Things will look brighter in the morning.'

He did as he was told, but sleep refused to come.

Downstairs, Ruth was speaking to Bob.

'Basil has just reminded me that we have to make a decision about school when the autumn term comes. I suppose one of us will have to go and speak to the local headmaster, to see if they have room.'

'I'm certainly not going back to school!' Marina announced.

'I want you to stay on and get a good education, my girl,' said her father. 'I've always thought you might train for something worthwhile. Teaching, say, or nursing.'

'No, Dad! As soon as I'm old enough, I'm joining the Wrens. That's if the war isn't over before then.'

'No daughter of mine . . . ' he roared, but Ruth motioned to him to calm down.

'We'll discuss this later,' she said, aware that Mamgu was watching this little family disagreement with interest. 'But if we do let you leave school — and I'm not saying that we will, mind — you needn't think you'll be sitting around here all day, filing your fingernails. You'll have to get a job to tide you over. It's about time you contributed something towards your keep.'

'Aw, Mum!' Marina pouted, dismayed by this unwelcome new idea.

★　★　★

'This won't be much of a picnic without decent food,' Marina complained to her mother. 'Remember when I was little? When we had that outing to Whipsnade Zoo and we took all that food? Pork pies, chocolate cake, egg sandwiches. And bananas!'

'And you fed your banana to one of the monkeys.' Ruth smiled. 'What I wouldn't give to taste a banana now! One day we'll have all that again, just you wait and see. Meanwhile you'll just have to make do with what we can spare.'

'But lettuce sandwiches, Mum! Really!' Marina sidled into the shop, where the remains of a large round cheese sat on the counter, waiting to be sliced up with a wire and weighed out for some lucky customer.

'Give us a bit of that cheese, Dad,' she wheedled. 'I need something to liven up these sandwiches.'

'You've had your ration for the week, my girl. It's not my fault if you've eaten it all at once.'

'Two ounces! It's hardly more than a mouthful. Isn't there anything else, then?'

She wandered around the shop, looking at the shelves, but everything she fancied took 'points'.

Bob ignored her. He was busy weighing out sugar into small blue bags so as to save time when customers came in to buy it. He was surprised that his daughter hadn't given him more of an argument but instead she rushed off, saying that she didn't want to keep Marged waiting.

He wasn't to know that two young men were hovering around the corner, watching for her arrival.

* * *

'So, what's so special about this famous mountain?' Marina asked Marged as they all set off.

'We're going up to the *gorsedd*,' Marged explained.

'What's that?'

'You'll see when we get there,' Tim told her.

It was a stiff climb up the hillside, and Marina fell into step beside Tim, leaving Marged and Emlyn to follow on. This, of course, suited Marged very well.

At last they reached the summit, and the whole town lay below them, looking like some toy village. Over to one side, the brooding colliery and the ugly slag heaps marred the landscape, while on the other, green fields, dotted with sheep, presented an illusion of peace. At that moment the war seemed very far away.

'And this is the *gorsedd*!' Emlyn announced proudly. 'I bet you don't have anything like this where you come from!'

Marina gazed in awe at the circle of giant stones. It reminded her of pictures she'd seen of Stonehenge, but on a smaller scale.

'I suppose this is where the druids came to worship,' she said. 'How on earth did they get these rocks up here? They must weigh a ton!'

The idea of hundreds of people — slaves, probably — pushing these great slabs up the mountainside was mind-boggling, to say the least. She said as much to Tim, who shrugged.

'The old people around here say that these aren't ancient stones at all. They were put here in the last century, when there was a revival of Welsh culture. There may have been druids in traditional robes performing their ceremonies here, but they were ordinary men, not mysterious beings from the dark ages.'

'Oh.' Marina was a little disappointed, but it still provided a topic of conversation, and she didn't want to appear tongue-tied in front of him. 'It still must have been difficult, setting all this up. Did they use horses, or what?'

But Tim was tired of the subject. 'Come on, let's put our food on the flat rock in the middle and share what we have. What did Mam give us, Marged?'

'Welsh cakes — with about one currant in each — and *tarten gennin*.' Marged smiled, and reached into her basket. 'That's leek flan to you, Marina. What did you bring, Emlyn?'

Emlyn's jaw dropped. 'I didn't know I was supposed to bring anything. You didn't say.'

'Emlyn Richards! You're stupid, you are!'

'When people ask you to tea, they don't say bring your own food. What's different about picnics?'

'In case you hadn't noticed, most people take something with them these days when they're invited out for a meal, so that other people don't have to dip into their own rations. Now we've got four people to feed on barely enough for three!'

'You didn't say!' he insisted.

Tight-lipped, Marged turned her back on him, but Marina noticed that, when it was time to divide up the *tarten*, Emlyn received a generous slice while Marged made do with a much smaller piece herself.

Marina herself was being watched with interest by Tim. Until now he had thought of her as a schoolgirl, but today she seemed much older. Dressed in a fresh gingham frock, topped with a white cardigan borrowed from her mother, she seemed to be closer to his own age. Perhaps it was because of her hair, which she was wearing loose instead of in her usual plaits.

These days, since the argument over the picnic, there was a distinct coolness between himself and Catrin Harris. Perhaps there was no harm in him getting to know Marina a little better. Nothing too serious, of course, but then, she wouldn't expect anything like that, would she? One of these days, she'd be going back to England and that would be the end of it. Ships that pass in the night.

'There's a hop in the Town Hall next Saturday night, Marina. Want to go?' he asked.

'Oh, yes, please,' she breathed. 'I'd love to.'

'Will your da let you?' Marged was doubtful.

'I'm sure I can talk him round.'

Nothing short of a miracle would make Bob Greene say yes, but Marina was not about to admit that in front of Tim. If necessary, she'd slip out of the house to go to the dance, and face the music later!

'I've got a better idea,' Marged said, understanding this without needing to be told. 'I'll get Mam to ask him, shall I?'

While Marged's mother had strong principles when it came to how girls should behave, she did at least allow her daughter to take part in such blameless pleasures that the town afforded.

'I've got nothing to wear,' Marina said, worried.

'Oh, that's all right. Nobody dresses up. Just wear an ordinary skirt and blouse. And don't bother about stock-ings, either. They're too precious to waste on a hop. All the girls wear ankle socks. So, do you want me to talk to Mam, or not?'

* * *

Bessie Parry picked her moment to mention the dance. She arrived at the house just as the Greenes were finishing their evening meal.

'I've brought that pattern you wanted to borrow, Mrs Greene. It should knit up lovely. Did you get that old grey jumper unpicked yet?'

'I don't know what you wanted to go and do that for,' Bob mumbled through a mouthful of scone. 'I always liked you in that.'

'Oh, Bob! I've darned the elbows so many times that there's more darn than sleeve! I'm going to knit it up again with short sleeves, from this new pattern.'

'No need for that, love! You could just re-do the sleeves. No need to change the whole thing.'

'You're missing the point, dear! I'm sick to death of the old rag. Mrs Parry's pattern has a pretty stitch in it. That'll make a change, and that's what I'm determined to have!'

Bessie saw that it was time to change the subject. She turned to speak to Marina. 'Are you going to the hop this Saturday, pet?'

'Um, I don't know, Mrs Parry. I'd really like to, but . . . '

'Marina doesn't go to dances,' Bob announced. 'It's kind of you to think of her, but she's far too young for that sort of thing.'

'This isn't exactly a dance, Mr Greene. It's just some of our young people getting together to shuffle around to gramophone records. It's well supervised, and there's certainly no drinking or anything wicked like that. I'm letting our Marged go.'

'I don't know . . . '

Bessie played her trump card. 'I'll be sending our Tim with them. He'll keep his eye on them, he will.'

'Go on, Bob, where's the harm?' Ruth smiled. 'If it makes you feel any better you can deliver the girls to the hall yourself, and fetch them home afterwards.'

'Mum!' Marina groaned.

'Well, if Tim is definitely going, I'm sure I can trust him to look after the girls. All right, then, I'll say yes, but you're to be home by nine, mind.'

'Nine? Dad! But it goes on until ten!'

'That's my last word, my girl! Take it or leave it.'

The problem was, of course, that whoever you had the last dance with was also the person who walked you home, and Marina was determined that that should be Tim Parry!

Marina was about to argue, but then her mother caught her eye.

'Leave this to me,' Ruth mouthed.

Troubled Times

'So give me all the news! I'm so bored, sitting here. Now I know how Mamgu feels. At least I've got hope that I'll be back on my feet in a few weeks. She could be lying around for the rest of her days,' said Dora, when Ruth next went to visit her.

'Then that's where you're wrong. She's been sitting in the kitchen with us, *and* she's muttering about going into the shop to give Bob a hand.'

'I don't believe it! How did that come about?'

'Bob used his charm on her, that's what. I just don't understand it, Dora. Here's me, dancing attendance on her, all sweetness and light, and it's like water off a duck's back. All Bob has to do is get masterful and she not only does what he says, but is all smiles with it.'

'It's because he's a man, Ruth. Women of her generation were brought up to think that men always know what's best. I bet Bob laps it up.'

'He does rather,' Ruth agreed. 'Still, in this case he seems to have known what he was doing. Your mother-in-law is much happier, and I don't have to run around with trays any more.'

The ward seemed a happier place, too, today. It appeared that Sister was off duty for a couple of days and a young blonde woman, known as 'Staff', was in charge in the interim. The young nurses bustled about, singing as they went, and even the bedclothes seemed more relaxed. When Sister was present everyone was tucked in so tightly that not a wrinkle could be seen in the blue bedspreads.

'At least she can't fasten me down, not with my leg strung up like this,' Dora said when Ruth remarked on this. 'Honestly, does it really matter whether the sheets are straight or not? You should be here when Matron's round is coming up. Everything has to be really shipshape by then. Even the wheels on the beds have to face in a certain direction.'

'Speaking of ships . . . '

'Before you ask, no, I haven't heard from Dai. I don't suppose any letters have come to the house?'

'No. I'd have handed anything over at once.'

Dora wiped a tear from her eye. 'I've written, of course, giving him my address here, but I haven't heard a thing this week. Every time they bring the post round I keep my fingers crossed, and then I'm disappointed, knowing I have to get through another twenty-four hours before there's another chance.'

Ruth didn't know what to say. The life of a merchant seaman was hard enough in the normal way of things, but in wartime it was even more fraught with danger. The dreaded U-boats with their torpedoes were prowling under the sea like giant sharks, dealing out death and destruction.

And Dora's son, Idris, in the Royal Navy, was in danger, too, although neither Ruth nor his mother knew exactly what he was up to, or even where he was, because those matters were kept secret in case the enemy latched on to the information.

'What about your lot?' Dora asked, pulling herself together with an effort. 'All right, are they?'

'Oh, yes. Bob's in his element in the shop. In fact, he's talking about us getting a little shop ourselves after the war. He enjoys being his own boss and he's getting to know all the customers. Do you know, a woman came in for her cheese ration the other day, and asked for a single ounce. 'But you're entitled to two ounces, Mrs Richards,' says Bob.

' 'Oh, I know, Mr Greene', she says, 'but if I take it now, I know I'll eat it all at once. If you keep some of it here, then I'll have something to look forward to, see?' '

'Poor Mrs Richards. She's another

one with a son at sea. An ounce of cheese! Honestly, that would be funny if it wasn't so awful. What do you miss the most, Ruth?'

Ruth had to think. 'Being able to have a heaped teaspoonful of sugar in my tea. That saccharin just isn't the same. And crumpets, with lashings of butter seeping through on to the plate.'

'Oh, stop it, do! You're making my mouth water.'

'Well, you did ask! Anyway, back to what we were saying before — Marina is on cloud nine over some hop the youngsters are going to on Saturday night.'

'No! You mean Bob's going to let her go?'

'Yes, but not without a great deal of fuss. He doesn't want her jitterbugging with a lot of lads she hasn't even been introduced to.'

'Dear old Bob.' Dora laughed. 'I don't think the Methodists do much jitterbugging. This will be far more sedate — foxtrotting about, with the chaperones telling the youngsters not to dance too close together, and the minister's wife standing at the door in case couples try to go outside to smooch!'

'Speaking of chaperones,' Ruth said, giggling, 'Bob wanted young Basil to go to the dance with Marina, to keep an eye on her! Well, Marina was having none of it, as you would expect, but it was Basil who surprised me. He got really angry. He shouted something about not being a spy, and that he hated the lot of us. Then he raced upstairs and slammed his bedroom door so hard that I was surprised it didn't come off its hinges. Bob and I were amazed. That's not like Basil at all.'

'Kids! Who knows what goes on in their minds? So, what's Bob going to do now?'

'He was still harping on about delivering the poor girl to the dance himself, but I think Bessie Parry's finally talked him out of that by saying that her son will look after both Marina and Marged. I'm afraid Marina has a crush on Tim, though. I hope it won't lead to anything or the fat will really be in the fire.'

'Oh, no, it certainly won't.' Dora shook her head decisively. 'Tim's courting Catrin Harris, that I do know.'

'Catrin Harris?'

'A girl his own age. You see that woman three beds down? In the blue bed-jacket? That's Catrin's auntie. She comes for a natter with me sometimes. She thoroughly approves of Tim Parry. He's got a steady job, one he'll probably have for life, *and* he doesn't have to go away to war.'

'Mining can be a pretty dangerous occupation, though.'

'True, but you can't go through life worrying about what could happen. If you had the safest job in the world it wouldn't stop you being hit by a bus or something. You know what they say about having to go when your number's up.'

Ruth shivered. 'Ooh, this is a morbid conversation! Let's change the subject. Tell me about all these other women in the ward. What's wrong with them, do you know?'

Dora, it seemed, knew about everyone's ailments. There was little Mrs Prior, who had practically starved herself by giving most of her rations to her young children. She had lost so much weight that the doctors believed she must have some awful disease — until they found out what she'd been doing. Now they were keeping her in hospital so that she could build up her strength again.

'Although what's the betting that once they let her out she'll go on just as she did before?'

'You can understand it though, can't you?' Ruth pointed out. 'At least my kids are old enough to understand what rationing means, even if they do grumble. It must be terribly hard if you have little ones crying for second helpings when there isn't enough to go round in the first place. It would break my heart.'

On the way home, Ruth considered what she had learned about Tim Parry. It was a relief to know that he was seeing someone his own age and was unlikely to be interested in Marina. No doubt the Harris girl would be at the dance, and Marina would see them together and realise there was no chance for her. After that there would be high drama, and Ruth would be left to pick up the pieces.

Basil Finds A Friend

Emrys Rees was a retired miner. Since the death of his wife from cancer, shortly after the outbreak of war, he had kept himself to himself, not wanting to mingle with his fellow man. He seldom went to the Red Dragon, and when former workmates greeted him on the street he responded with a curt 'Bore da' and walked on.

It had been a great sorrow to Glynis Rees that she and Emrys hadn't been blessed with children, and there had been a time when her husband agreed with her, but not now. Any family they had had would have been caught up in the war now, at best serving in faraway places, at worst possibly being killed or maimed.

But Emrys was fond of children, although he knew few of them very well. And so, when he caught sight of a small boy hanging around the allotments, he was intrigued.

He noted that the child wore a faded grey shirt, and shorts that had been bought too large, to allow for growth. In that regard, his appearance was much the same as most local boys in these days of clothes rationing, but something marked this child out as being different. Emrys was unable to put his finger on what it was, but it was there.

Perhaps it was a lack of confidence, a feeling of being out of place somehow?

Emrys knew that feeling. He'd felt like that himself, ever since Glynis had passed on.

'*Bore da!*' Emrys called.

The boy looked up and came closer to where Emrys was adjusting his bean poles.

'Sorry, sir, I can't speak Welsh.'

'English, is it? That's what we'll use, then.'

Everybody in Bedwen spoke both languages, except for some of the very old people, who preferred to use Welsh all the time, even though — or perhaps because — they'd been forced to learn English at the school.

In the old days, when Queen Victoria was on the throne, their native tongue had even been banned in the classroom and the playground, the idea being that anyone who wished to get on in the world needed to be able to converse in the first language of the Empire.

A lot of nonsense, Emrys had always thought; it didn't matter what language a man spoke when he was down the pit.

'Would you like a carrot?' He pulled one out of the ground and dusted it clean on his moleskin trousers.

'Thanks.' Basil accepted the offering and began to crunch it between small white teeth.

'Not playing with your mates today, then?'

'No, I haven't got any.'

Emrys blinked.

'Well, that's awful! Surely there must be somebody who'd give you a game of football? Or is it cricket you play, you being English? Not much call for that round by here, see? Where are you from, then?' he asked, and was taken aback at the change that came over the boy.

'I'm not a spy! My dad's not a spy!' Basil shouted, clenching his fists.

'Nobody said you were, *bach*!'

'You would if I said where I was from, and I won't tell you, so there!'

Emrys debated with himself whether to explore this further, or to leave well alone. Children got hold of some funny ideas at times.

However, he considered himself to be a good judge of people and he sensed that the boy was almost at breaking point, so he decided to risk it.

'What's wrong, *bach*? Why don't you tell me what's up? It may be that I can help. Two heads are better than one, they say.'

As Basil burst out crying, Emrys reached over and patted him on the back.

'If things are that bad, you'd better tell your mam and dad about it, eh?'

'I can't!' the boy sobbed. 'If I say anything they'll send my father to prison, and we'll never see him again. What if they shoot him or something?'

What in the name of goodness had the man done? The last thing Emrys wanted was to get involved in something dodgy. It came to him then that these must be the people who were standing in for Dora Thomas at the shop. He'd never met the man; was it possible that he was dealing on the black market and putting the stuff through the shop? The Thomas family were stalwarts of the chapel. They would never get over the shame. Still, something urged Emrys to probe further.

'What makes you think your da could go to prison,' he asked carefully.

Basil stared back at his new friend, searching his face as if trying to decide whether he could be trusted.

'It's the boys. The ones I was playing

with. They said my father's a German spy. They said he's here to find out information to send to the enemy. It's a big fat lie, that's what it is!'

'That's just games, boyo. Having you on, they are.'

'No, sir, when I told them where we were from, they said that I was talking German, and I'm a spy. I said that was daft, and then they said it must be Dad.'

Emrys closed his eyes in exasperation. 'And where *are* you from, *bach*?'

'Hemel, sir. Hemel Hempstead really, only we always say just Hemel. It's a place in Hertfordshire, sir.'

This meant nothing to Emrys, and he couldn't see the connection with spying.

'Who was it started all this nonsense?'

'Rhodri, sir. I think his surname is Evans.'

'Oh, ay, I know the family. Well, you run along now, and let me have a bit of a think. Between the two of us, we should be able to make sense out of this.'

'You won't tell the police, will you?' Basil was still anxious.

'Na, na, you can trust me.'

Basil sped off, not altogether convinced.

Emrys sat on an upturned pail and took a pull on his pipe. He'd heard the tales about spies, and it was probably true that Britain had been infiltrated by enemy agents, just as the British were likely to be sending men and women into occupied territory abroad. All that was hush hush, of course, but it didn't take much of a brain to work out what was going on.

However, he was willing to bet that the people at the grocer's shop were in the clear. The woman — this boy's mother — was connected to Dora Thomas in some way, and they'd come to Bedwen to help out while Dora was in hospital, there being nobody else to take care of Mair Thomas in her absence. There was no way the enemy could have arranged all that!

* * *

Bessie Parry was amazed when she found Emrys standing on her doorstep. 'Emrys Rees. Fancy seeing you here! *Sut yr ydych chwi?*'

He agreed that he was well enough.

Sitting at Bessie's kitchen table, he fumbled for the right words.

'These people up at the shop. All right, are they?'

'All right? Oh, they're very healthy, so far as I know.'

'Na, na, *merch*. What I mean is, can they be trusted?'

Bessie bridled. 'I don't know what you're getting at, Emrys Rees, but they seem decent enough to me, coming all this way from London to help poor Dora.'

'Not London. The little chap said something about a place called Hemel.'

'That will be Basil. What's all this about, then?'

Emrys had known Bessie for years and decided he could trust her.

'It's those boys, Rhodri Evans in particular. They've got it into their heads that these people at the shop are enemy agents, and the boy is being made to suffer for it.'

'Stuff and nonsense! Well, there's only one thing to do. Even if the child has sworn you to secrecy, you must go and speak to Bob Greene and let him deal with it. These things have a habit of snowballing if they're not nipped in the bud.'

Despite her mixed metaphors, Bessie was talking sense, and within minutes, Emrys found himself in the little shop, facing Basil's father over the counter.

'What can I do for you, sir?'

Emrys looked around cautiously. 'Your little boy isn't within earshot, is he?'

'Basil? No, he's running an errand for my wife. Why, what's he been up to?'

Emrys plunged straight into his story, and was taken aback when Bob guffawed.

'Kids! What will they think of next?'

'I think this is a bit more serious, Mr Greene. Oh, I'm sure the constable won't be marching you off in handcuffs just yet, but your boy is extremely distressed by all this. And it can only get worse as time goes on. He can stay away from the other children now, but once school starts again they'll have him where they want him. It could come to blows.'

'Then what do you think I ought to do?'

'Call on Gareth Evans, Rhodri's father, when you get a moment. He's a reasonable man. He'll help you to sort this out.'

The two men shook hands as Emrys took his leave.

*　　*　　*

'Anyone for a game of Snap, or Happy Families?' Basil asked hopefully. Tea was over, his sister was clearing the table, and the shop was closed for the day. This was the time he liked best because if he was lucky, one or both of his parents would pay attention to him.

'Not now, Basil. You and I are going for a walk.'

Basil looked up at his father in surprise. 'But it's raining, Dad, coming down cats and dogs, and my mac is leaking. Can't we go for a walk tomorrow instead?'

Marina came in from the scullery just then and her father caught her eye.

'Go upstairs for a bit, love. Would you mind? Or if you'd rather, go in and chat to Mamgu. I want to have a word with your brother in private.'

Raising her eyes to the ceiling, Marina did as she was told. She'd known for days that the kid was up to something and now, whatever it was, he'd been caught out doing it. Would he never learn?

'You'd better hear this, too,' Bob told his wife. 'Come and sit down.'

'Can't it wait? I've got a sink full of pots, and now that you've sent Marina off, I'll be stuck doing them all myself.'

'They'll still be there when we've finished.'

'That's what I'm afraid of,' she retorted.

Basil felt like screaming. Why couldn't they just get on with it, whatever it was? He twisted his features into what he hoped was an angelic expression.

'It has come to my attention,' Bob began, putting on what Ruth thought of as his pompous manner, 'that some boys have been saying some very silly things to you.'

'What sort of things, Bob?' asked Ruth.

Basil had gone white and his mother didn't like the look of him. This sounded serious.

'Well, Basil? What have you got to say to us?'

'Nothing, Dad.'

'Are you sure about that?'

'Yes, Dad.'

'Then I must tell you that I know all about it.'

'If you know all about it, then what

are you asking me for?' his son burst out.

'Don't be cheeky, lad. I wanted to hear your side of the story before taking action. Now, is this right? Rhodri Evans and some other boys think we're enemy agents because we're not Welsh, is that it?'

Ruth gasped. 'What rubbish! They can't have come to that conclusion just because we're English! We're all Britons, aren't we? All in this together? Oh, whoever started this crazy talk deserves a good clip round the ear!'

'I don't think it's because we're English, Mum, and it wasn't really Rhodri. It was his dad that said we were Germans, not him. Unless Rhodri's fibbing, of course.'

'Well, I'm going to get to the bottom of this before I'm much older. I'm going round to see this man — Gareth Evans his name is — and I'm going to have it out with him.'

'Dad, no!'

'Oh, yes, I am, and you're coming

with me, so don't give me any more of your lip. Get your mac on, leaky or not, and we'll go and get it over with.'

'You will be careful, won't you, Bob? Don't do anything you might regret.' Ruth's hands were tightly clenched inside her apron pocket as she spoke.

'I'm not about to punch him, if that's what you mean,' said Bob.

★　★　★

Gareth Evans greeted them pleasantly enough, and ushered them into a kitchen that was very similar to their own. Despite the fact that it was midsummer, the air was chilly from the damp, and there was a fire burning in the grate.

Bob sat down on the chair that was pulled out for him, and Basil stood at his father's shoulder, ready to run if it should become necessary.

'We haven't been introduced, but I've seen you in the Red Dragon, Mr Greene. Now, what can I do for you?

My wife hasn't been asking you for tick at the shop, has she? I know Dora Thomas doesn't allow that.'

'Nothing like that, Mr Evans. The fact is, there seems to be a bit of a problem between your boy and mine. This is rather awkward, but your lad's been putting it about that I'm a spy, some sort of German agent, and the other children are giving Basil here a rough time over it.'

Rhodri's father smothered a grin, but realising the seriousness of the accusation, quickly pulled himself together.

'You're sure about this, boy? Perhaps they were talking Welsh and you got the wrong end of the stick.'

'Yes, sir. I mean, I didn't get the wrong idea; that's what they said.'

'And furthermore,' Bob put in, 'your son seems to have been acting on something you said about all this.'

'Has he indeed! Well, we'll see what he's got to say for himself now! Rhodri!'

Rhodri came clattering down from

upstairs, only to stop short when he saw Basil, accompanied by a strange man.

'What's all this I hear about you accusing Mr Greene here of being a spy?'

'Well, he could be, Da. We're always hearing about how we should watch out for spies. It said so on the wireless, and the *Meistr* told us that at school as well.'

'Listen here, boyo,' said Rhodri's father sternly, 'I know you've never set foot outside this town, but there's one thing you've got to learn. There are lots of people in the world who are on our side. Just because Mr Greene isn't a Welshman, doesn't mean he's with the enemy!'

'Oh, I know that, Da, I'm not stupid. But it was you who told me they're Germans.'

'What? I did not! What's the matter with you, boy?'

'You did, Da! I asked Basil where he's from and he said Hemel.'

'So what?'

'And you said that's what the Germans call Heaven. You did, Da, you did! And it was you that told me ages ago about everybody coming from Heaven when they're born, so if Basil came from the German part of Heaven — well, that's suspicious, see?'

Gareth Evans groaned. 'I seem to remember you asking me something like that,' he said, 'but I didn't pay much attention because I was trying to hear the nine o'clock news. I thought you said Himmel, see? Himmel!'

Rhodri's face was blank, and Basil merely looked bewildered.

'I see it all, now!' Bob laughed. 'I expect you said Hemel, didn't you, Basil? We're from Hemel Hempstead, Rhodri, a small town not far from London. It's thoroughly British, and so are we.'

Mr Evans nodded.

'So there you are, son. It doesn't pay to jump to conclusions. Next time, come to me first if you think you've found a nest of spies. Now, I expect you've something to say to Basil here, haven't you?'

Rhodri shuffled his feet before muttering an insincere, 'Sorry!'

'I must apologise for all this, Mr Greene,' said Gareth Evans. 'If only I'd realised what was going on, I'd have put a stop to it at once. My wife is a close friend of Dora Thomas, see. Visits her up at the hospital, she does. Very grateful to you for coming to stay, Dora is. I tell you what we'll do.' Gareth Evans beamed. 'To make it up to you, Basil, you can come here to tea on Sunday. How will that be?'

'That's very kind,' Bob told him, when it became clear that Basil wasn't going to respond. 'I'll see that my wife sends a bit of something to eat along with him.'

'Na, na! If there's not enough to go round, our Rhodri can go short for once. It'll save me sending him to bed without his supper as punishment for all this upset that's been caused.'

And with that the whole nasty

business came to an end. Satisfied, the two men shook hands.

The cold lump which had settled on Basil's stomach ever since this terror began was now starting to dissipate. At the same time it was with a sharp sensation of guilt that it occurred to him that, lurking in the far reaches of his mind, there had been a tiny suspicion that his father might have been in league with the enemy after all.

He knew he would never be able to forgive himself for that, and he would certainly never forgive Rhodri and his henchmen.

He wanted to cry out that he hadn't really thought such a thing, and certainly never would. The idea had just crawled unbidden into his mind.

Yet young as he was, he knew he must never tell anyone about this, or his father would be hurt beyond belief, and he couldn't bear that.

Trapped!

Ruth felt quite sentimental as, that Saturday night, she waved her daughter off on her way to the hop.

'Just think, our little girl is going to her first dance!' she said softly. 'Oh, Bob, they grow up so fast, don't they?'

'Too fast!' he grunted.

'Remember our dancing days? How they used to spread soap flakes all over the dance floor to make it slippery and easier to glide across?'

'They won't be doing that tonight, old girl. Soap flakes are as scarce as snowballs at the equator as it is, never mind wasting them on such foolishness. Switch on the wireless while you're on your feet. I could do with a bit of music.'

The comforting voice of Vera Lynn, the Forces' Sweetheart, filled the room. Ruth sang along with her: 'There'll be bluebirds over, the white cliffs of Dover, tomorrow, just you wait and see . . . '

'Can I go out, Mum?' Basil interrupted.

'Out? Where do you want to go at this time of night?'

'It's only seven o'clock, Mum.'

'Didn't you hear me? I said, where do you want to go?'

'Down to the Town Hall, to see what they're doing. I want to watch them going in.'

'I can't imagine what for. It'll just be a few boys and girls dressed in their ordinary clothes, going to play a few records and have a dance about. Not like in my young day, when we knew how to do things properly.'

'Mum!'

'Oh, let the boy go,' Bob groaned. 'Anything for a bit of peace and quiet. What's the point of having the wireless on, if I'm not allowed to listen to it?'

'Well, go on then, Basil,' said Ruth, 'but you're to be back here no later than eight o'clock, do you hear me?'

'Yes, Mum.' Basil sped off before his parents could change their minds.

He deeply resented the fact that he had to go to bed at eight o'clock. It wasn't so bad in winter, when the evenings were dark and cold and it was a pleasure to huddle under the blankets, but summer was different. He would lie there, tossing and turning while the sun was still shining outside, and he could hear the shouts of luckier children playing in the distance. But no matter how much he pleaded to stay up later, his mother was adamant. He was a growing boy, and he needed his sleep.

* * *

But Basil wasn't on his way to the Town Hall because he was interested in the dancers. No, he was more interested in what they might have to eat.

Basil had been to tea at Rhodri's home, as arranged, and had enjoyed playing bagatelle, a game which was new to him.

When they had tired of this the two boys had sat on the stairs, talking.

'Are you going to the hop?' Rhodri had asked.

'Of course not. It's stupid. You might have to talk to girls.'

'Ah, but they're having food.'

'What sort of food?'

'Pop and biscuits, I think. Last time, they had spam sandwiches.'

'How do you know?' Basil said, his voice full of scorn.

'My cousin Catrin was here. I heard her telling Mam. She goes to the hop with Tim Parry, Catrin does. The thing is, they keep the food in the back room until half-time. And I know where there's a little window. We can get inside and help ourselves.'

Basil tried not to look shocked. 'Wouldn't that be stealing?'

'Na, na. It's for everybody who goes to the hop, see? We wouldn't take it all, just a little bit. They'd never miss it. Stands to reason — they don't know how many people to provide for.'

'Well, if you think nobody would mind . . . '

Basil's mouth watered at the thought of sinking his teeth into a spam sandwich, and how long was it since he'd tasted orange pop? It didn't occur to him to wonder why — if the food was there for everyone — it would be necessary for them to climb in through a window.

'I'll meet you there, then,' Rhodri grinned. 'Seven-fifteen, sharp. That gives the ladies time to put out the food, see?'

When Basil had gone home, Rhodri told himself that his plan was foolproof. He'd help the other boy through the window and then run off, leaving him to face the music.

Rhodri was still smouldering over the episode of the spies. So, he'd been wrong about the Greenes; what of it? It was everyone's patriotic duty to keep on the look-out for stuff like that. People should have been pleased with his efforts.

Mr Greene had been a sport. He hadn't shouted, or asked for Rhodri to be punished, and even Da had said 'boys will be boys' and said they'd let it go this once.

It was Mam who'd jumped on him like a ton of bricks.

'That poor young boy!' she'd gasped. 'Imagine what you've put him through. It's a sharp lesson you need, boyo!'

The lesson had come only that morning, when he'd had to miss the Saturday matinee at the pictures. Mam had refused to give him the empty jam jar which — if you didn't have the necessary tuppence — was the price of admission to the cinema.

Fuming, he'd decided that he had to make Basil suffer too.

* * *

When Basil reached the High Street, it was to see a number of young people heading for the Town Hall, girls arm in

146

arm, boys slouching along in small groups.

Spotting Rhodri loitering in the doorway of the draper's shop, Basil hurried to join him.

'Duck down!' Rhodri hissed. 'Don't let anybody see us!'

Basil couldn't see that it mattered, but he entered into the spirit of the game until the last of the dancers had disappeared inside the hall. Then the pair of them darted along the deserted street.

'Round the back!' Rhodri ordered, leading the way to a small window set high in the wall. It was the sort which had to be opened from the bottom, and someone had already pushed it up by about three or four inches.

'All clear!' Rhodri whispered. 'Come on, I'll give you a bunk up.'

'How will you get in, then?'

'I won't need to. You pass the stuff out to me, and then you come back out yourself.'

Boosted up by Rhodri, Basil scrambled

through the window, grazing himself painfully on the knee as he fell off the sill.

He hesitated beside the table where the food was set out. No sandwiches, but there were some stale-looking rock cakes and several bottles of pop.

At that moment, Basil heard voices from the other side of the door.

'It's good of you to bring jam tarts, Mrs Griffiths. The young people will be grateful, I'm sure.'

'It's only that awful imitation stuff with parsnips in it,' the invisible Mrs Griffiths replied. 'Still, it's better than nothing, I suppose.'

In a panic, Basil looked for an escape route. He knew he couldn't reach the window without help, and there wasn't any sort of box or chair he could use, even if he'd had time to put it in place.

Looking around wildly, he wrenched open a nearby door, slipping inside in the nick of time. It was a deep cupboard with shelves on three sides, stacked with box files and heavy ledgers. His heart pounding, he sank down on the floor.

'Just put them on the table, Mrs Griffiths. You can come and fetch your plate later. I believe you're one of the chaperones for this evening? How can you stand that horrid jazz music? Give me a nice bit of opera any day.'

'They could hardly dance to Rigoletto!' the other woman laughed, but she was rudely interrupted by a snort of outrage from her companion.

'Well, really! They've left this cupboard with the key in the lock, and all the important council papers inside! I'll hand the key over to Councillor Morgan, and give him a piece of my mind with it!'

There was a loud click, after which the footsteps receded, and Basil was left alone in the dark. He fumbled for the handle but it wouldn't turn.

He was locked in.

★　★　★

Inside, the hall was full of people, but nobody was dancing. The girls were standing about in small groups, talking with false animation — pretending not to notice the boys — while the young men in question leaned against the wall and eyed the girls.

'There's Emlyn,' Marina whispered. 'I wonder if he's going to ask you to dance, Marged? Shall I wave to him? He might come over.'

'Don't you dare!' Marged hissed. 'I don't want him to think I'm fast! Better to wait till everybody's dancing.'

'I wouldn't want to be first on the floor, either,' Marina told her. 'I'd be mortified to have everyone looking at me. That's if anyone asks me to dance at all,' she added.

'Oh, don't worry!' Marged hastened to reassure her. 'They always have a Paul Jones to get everybody mingling, and if that fails, Tim will dance with you.'

Before leaving home, Marged had punched her brother on the arm and warned him that if he didn't give Marina a dance or two, she'd never speak to him again.

'It's the least you can do when the poor girl is a stranger here,' she'd told Tim, and their mother, coming into the room in time to hear this, had agreed.

'I promised Mrs Greene you'd watch out for that girl of hers, our Tim, so mind you don't make a liar out of me.'

'I may, or I may not, Mam. That's the best I can say.'

It all depended on whether Catrin was at the dance, Tim told himself. Naturally, she would expect him to dance with her. That was the whole point of being part of a courting couple; you had someone to go to social events with.

Unfortunately for Catrin, she arrived at the hall in the company of her next-door neighbour, Harry Lloyd. It wasn't her fault that they both happened to be heading in the same direction. Besides, she'd always liked Harry. They'd known each other since they were toddlers and Catrin thought of him as an adopted brother.

Strolling along the street behind Marina and his sister, Tim saw Catrin and Harry arriving together. Catrin smiled at Harry as they reached the door, and he took her by the elbow to steer her inside. Neither of them noticed Tim, whose face turned red with annoyance.

'Why, isn't that your Catrin?' Marged asked him brightly.

'You know very well it is!' Tim growled. 'And don't call her *my* Catrin!'

'But I thought the two of you were going together?' Marged asked innocently, winking at Marina. 'Are you going to land one on Harry Lloyd's nose?'

'I don't care what she does. We're not married. She's free to please herself.'

Marina was delighted. Her pleasure at coming to the dance with the Parrys had been tempered by the knowledge that if Catrin were present, then Tim would gravitate to her and Marina wouldn't get a look-in. Now, if she played her cards right, he might turn his attention to herself after all.

Catrin saw the trio entering the hall. She frowned at the sight of the pretty girl at Tim's side. How dare he turn up with somebody else? It was bad enough that he hadn't offered to call for her at home.

Not for the first time, she wondered what had gone wrong between them. What had she done that was so terrible?

When her friend, Gwyneth, had invited her to go to the pictures to see 'For Me And My Gal', she'd accepted without a second thought. That sort of film wasn't Tim's cup of tea at all. Far better to go with Gwyn, even if it meant paying for themselves. Why couldn't Tim understand instead of taking the huff because she wasn't free to go on some old picnic up the mountain with him?

Catrin glared across the room at him, but he wasn't looking in her direction.

Instead, he was talking to that simpering English girl.

Now the music was playing loudly, and several couples were moving happily in time to the beat. Marina was thrilled when Tim asked her to dance. She hadn't much experience, but he steered her expertly across the floor and he didn't tread on her toes once.

There was a break while the record was changed, and then he led her on to the floor again, taking it for granted that she'd be in agreement. She was blissfully unaware that he had one eye on Catrin Harris, who, to show that she didn't care, was chattering animatedly to a girl friend.

'Can we have a ladies' choice?' Catrin whispered to Gwil Jones, the elderly man in charge of changing the records. He was the Town Hall janitor in everyday life.

'In a minute, *bach*. Wait till I get a slow one going. Is that all right?'

Catrin nodded. That would give her time to decide whether to ask some other boy to dance so as to make Tim jealous, or to go over and drag him off from under that awful Marina's nose.

Out of the corner of her eye she saw her cousin, Rhodri, edging his way into the hall. What was he doing slinking around like that? This dance was for the over sixteens, no kids allowed. Besides, what was he doing, out at night? According to Catrin's mother, the boy had been up to mischief of some sort and was being punished.

Rhodri edged his way towards the room where the snacks were laid out. It was one thing to urge Basil into mischief but quite another not to know what had happened to him. Not that his conscience was troubling him, he just needed to have his story straight if questions were asked later.

'And where do you think you're going, boy?'

Rhodri recognised Mrs Phillips, a stern lady who played a part in many of the town's organisations, such as the Red Cross and the Friends of the

155

Library. She was not a person to be argued with.

'Just looking, I was, Mrs Phillips.'

'Then you can go just looking outside. There's nothing to see here.'

'What's in there?' he asked desperately, looking at the inner door.

'Nothing that need interest you. Off you go now, or I'll be having a word with your mam the next time I meet her.'

There was nothing for it but to leave the hall. But where could Basil be? Hiding, perhaps? Or had he been apprehended already and taken to the police station?

Out on the street Rhodri began to laugh. He'd played a good joke on that stupid Basil. This was turning out better than he'd hoped.

★　★　★

Inside the cupboard, Basil knelt on the linoleum-covered floor, listening to the throbbing of the music. He gave a tentative knock on the door, expecting it to be flung open by some irate person, but nobody came. He would have to wait until the crowd came in during the interval for refreshments.

He knew he was in big trouble. When he was eventually set free, questions would be asked. They would want to know what he was doing there.

Climbing into the Town Hall through a window had been a bad thing to do. He knew that now. At the time, it had seemed like an adventure, but that was not how his parents would see it. What would the authorities do to him? Would he have to go to court? At least he hadn't stolen anything, because there hadn't been time.

The music stopped, and suddenly the room was filled with voices as the young people crowded in, handing over their money and accepting their snacks. At one point Basil thought he recognised Marina's voice, and that stopped him from banging on the door again. If it was known that she was his sister, then she might be blamed, too.

Eventually the room beyond the cupboard door fell silent once more as the dancers returned to the hall and the music started up again.

An hour passed, although for Basil it seemed like an eternity. Finally, the music stopped altogether and he could hear the faint sounds of retreating footsteps and doors banging in the distance. The dance was over. Now he would shout for help.

'We'll come back in the morning and clear up the mess in there,' Mrs Phillips announced to Gwil Jones, who held the door open for her before locking up and leaving.

There was silence, and Basil was alone in the dark.

Where Is Basil?

'Where on earth is that boy?' Ruth looked at the clock for the fifth time in as many minutes. 'I told him he had to be back by eight o'clock. You heard me tell him that, didn't you, Bob?'

'What's that? Oh, yes. I expect he's lost track of the time. Look, it's time for the nine o'clock news; I can't miss that. Wait until it's over and then I'll go and have a look for him.'

He leaned over to switch on the wireless.

'This is the BBC Home Service,' the announcer said, in clipped tones.

Ruth got up to peer out of the kitchen window. For once she couldn't settle to listen to the news. It would be all doom and gloom as usual, with perhaps a bit of propaganda thrown in so that ordinary people wouldn't lose heart. Bob maintained that the government probably suppressed the news of some quite disastrous happenings for that very reason. This war was being waged on the home front as well as abroad.

But what was any of that, compared with a missing child? Basil should have been home an hour ago, and there was still no sign of him. Had he stayed out on purpose? It wasn't like him to be so naughty.

Ruth gave herself a mental shake. Bob was right, of course. The boy didn't possess a watch, and with these light evenings it would be easy to imagine that it was earlier than it was. Perhaps they'd left the door open at the Town Hall and he was gazing enthralled at the dancers. While that hardly seemed likely, what other explanation could there be?

The tinkling of a bell sounded from the parlour, warning her that Mamgu needed attention.

Ruth went in to see what the matter was.

'Sorry to bother you, Mrs Greene.

It's my Bible, see? Left it on top of the piano, I did, and I didn't want to fetch it myself.'

'No, indeed,' Ruth murmured. 'I don't think you're up to walking all the way across the room by yourself.'

'I like to read the Scriptures last thing at night,' Mamgu explained, accepting the leather-bound volume into her gnarled hands. 'Sort of settles me for sleep, see?'

'I could do with something to settle myself,' Ruth told her.

'Nothing wrong, is there?'

'No, no; it's just that the children aren't home yet. Marina has gone to that hop, as they call it, with the young Parrys.'

'I heard about that from Bessie. Your girl will be safe enough if her Tim has anything to do with it.'

'I expect so. It's my little boy I'm more worried about. He should have been home ages ago, but so far he hasn't turned up.'

Mamgu smiled. 'Boys will be boys!'

The two women were getting along much better these days. Mamgu seemed happier about their living arrangements since she'd been able to join the family in the kitchen, and Ruth had become used to the older woman's ways and was more tolerant of her foibles.

Now they chatted like old friends until Mamgu swallowed a yawn, and Ruth bid her goodnight.

When she returned to the kitchen the news was over and Bob was banking down the coal fire.

'It's just struck ten. They'll be coming out of the dance about now. Perhaps I'll take a stroll down the road to meet them. I could do with a stretch.'

'I'm coming with you, Bob. Just wait while I run up and fetch my cardigan.'

'No need for that, old girl. It's best you stay here, in case Basil turns up while I'm out. He'll be frightened if he comes in and finds us all missing.'

'I'll give him missing!' Ruth snapped, but she knew that what her husband said made sense. She happened to know that Basil hadn't yet recovered from all the worry of that silly spy scare. He'd had a nightmare in which his parents had been taken away by the police, and although she'd assured him it wasn't likely to happen, he hadn't been totally convinced. Children were such funny creatures. All sorts of strange ideas got into their heads.

* * *

Marina was feeling extremely pleased with herself. The dance had gone well and she'd spent a good deal of the evening with Tim. And even when she had been asked to dance by one or two other chaps, Tim hadn't gone near Catrin Harris. He'd even paid for Marina's drink, although she'd brought sixpence with her for the purpose.

Now they were strolling homeward in the balmy summer air, but Marged had linked arms with both Tim and Marina, so it was unlikely that a goodnight kiss was in the offing.

163

Still, it was fun to dream, and when they were standing outside her back door he might ask her to go out with him again.

These hopes were dashed when she saw her father striding towards them. How embarrassing! He'd promised faithfully that he wouldn't come to meet her like a child being collected at the school gates. She was sixteen years old! Didn't he trust her?

'Dad! What are you doing here?'

'Where's Basil? Isn't he with you?'

'Basil? Isn't he at home? Why should he be with us?'

'He went out earlier, saying he meant to walk up to the Town Hall to watch the folk going in. I couldn't see any harm in it, so we let him go. He was supposed to be back by eight, but so far there's no sign of him.'

'I'll come and help you search for him,' Tim volunteered at once. 'He'll be with some of his mates, and I know all the places where little boys like to go. I was young once!'

'You go home and tell your mother what's happening,' Bob ordered Marina, 'and before you ask, you can't come with us. Your mum's upset enough as it is, without worrying about you going missing as well.'

Marina shrugged and trotted off with Marged. What an end to her lovely evening! She could kill that young brother of hers.

Ruth was relieved to see her daughter but by this time she was near to tears.

'Dad said to tell you he's looking for Basil, and Tim Parry is going with him. You mustn't worry, Mum.'

'I mustn't worry, you say! Of course I must worry. Anything might have happened. He could have fallen into the river and drowned. He might even be at the bottom of a disused mine shaft somewhere!'

'Mum, Mum, calm down. The mine is miles away, and what would he be doing there anyhow?'

Marina wisely said nothing about the river. She happened to know that the boys spent many happy hours there, paddling or trying to fish. Basil hadn't played with them since that business with Rhodri, but what if he had wandered up there alone? He might have slipped on a wet rock and been swept away by the current.

'Shall we have a cup of tea while we're waiting, Mum?'

'Our ration's all gone,' Ruth told her.

Marina sighed. This blessed war! She couldn't even offer her mother a drop of tea to calm her nerves.

'I could go into the shop and borrow some against next week's ration. That wouldn't be wrong, would it?'

'Better not. Once we start that, we'll never catch up.'

Each person was allowed only two ounces of tea each week, which was nothing compared with pre-war con-sumption. Even when you reused the same tea leaves over and over again, it still wasn't enough.

Hunched over in their chairs to catch the remaining heat from the fire, the pair of them waited in silence for news.

Meanwhile, the two men marched through the town, passing the Town Hall — which was locked and deserted — on their way to the river.

'It's lucky you brought your torch, Mr Greene. It'll be almost dark when we get there. We're just going on the off-chance, mind. If anything had happened we'd have heard by now.'

'My thoughts exactly, but the river is the first place my wife will ask me about, and I'll be able to reassure her on that point at least.'

But the riverbank was deserted, and although Tim led the way to the recreation ground and the other places that Basil was most likely to be, it was as if the child had vanished off the face of the earth.

'I think we should fetch the police,' Tim said at last.

'Yes, I'm afraid we must,' Bob agreed, his face white.

Stretched out on the floor of the cupboard, Basil lay cold and alone.

* * *

'Do you mean to tell me there's no sign of him at all? Something must have happened to him. Oh, what are we going to do now?'

'Hush, you'll wake the old lady,' said Bob, putting his arm around his wife's shaking shoulders. 'Tim Parry has gone to alert the police. He'll be back at any moment with the constable.'

True to his word, Tim had gone to the constable's home and, although he was officially off duty, the man got up at once, reaching for his boots.

Llew Roberts was a stocky, dark-haired man with an air of confidence about him. He strode into the Greenes' kitchen as if he belonged there and sat himself down in front of the fire, which by now had blazed up again, having been stirred by Marina.

'No need to worry just yet,' he said easily. 'Little boys run away from home all the time, but they come back as soon as they get hungry. I did it myself when

168

I was this lad's age. Basil, you say his name is? Has he been worrying about anything lately? Or maybe he's been into mischief and doesn't want to come home for fear of what he'll face?'

'No,' Bob told him, just as Ruth chimed in with, 'Yes, he has.'

Llew looked from one to the other.

'So, which is it, then?'

Bob explained the trouble Basil had had with the other boys.

'But that's all behind us now. I've put a stop to it. The ringleader has been punished by his father, and I doubt he'll cause any more trouble now.'

'Basil went to tea with him only this afternoon,' Ruth put in.

'The ringleader, you say? Now who would that be?'

'A boy called Rhodri Evans.'

'Gareth Evans' boy?' asked Llew. 'I may as well have a word with him. He might just know something. Would you like to come along, Mr Greene?'

'I'm coming too!' Ruth cried, and this time there was no argument from her husband. The situation was so serious that no-one had the heart to keep her out of the picture.

'You'd better stay here, Marina, in case Mamgu rings,' she instructed.

'What'll I do if Basil shows up, then?'

'If that happens, you can see him into bed. We'll deal with him in the morning.'

'All right, Mum.' Marina noticed with a sinking feeling in her stomach that her mother had said 'if', not 'when'. It would be terrible if something dreadful had happened to her young brother. He could be an awful nuisance at times but, underneath it all, she loved him. Not that she'd ever tell him that!

★   ★   ★

'All right, all right! I'm coming!' Gareth Evans unlocked his front door and flung it open, amazed to see the quartet who were waiting on the doorstep. 'What's up, Llew? Not come to arrest me, have you?' He laughed uncertainly.

'Can we come in, man? This is official business, see?'

As they filed into the kitchen, Mrs Evans came down the stairs, tying the sash of her dressing-gown as she came. Her hair was done up in curlers and her face was smeared with cream.

'What's going on, Gareth?' she demanded to know.

'We need a word with your boy, Gareth,' said Llew. 'Basil Greene has gone missing. Looked everywhere, we have. Searched the whole town. We're hoping that Rhodri may be able to shed some light on it.'

'Of course he can't,' Mrs Evans bristled. 'He's in his bed. Your little boy came here to tea, Mr Greene, but he left hours ago. We haven't seen him since.'

'You may not have seen him,' Llew corrected, 'but what about Rhodri? Did he go out to play after tea?'

'Well, he did go up to the Rec for a bit. No harm in that, is there?'

'No harm at all, Mrs Evans.'

'Oh, can't we all stop beating about the bush like this?' Ruth cried. 'Can't you see we're wasting time? Basil could be lying injured somewhere. We simply must find him as soon as possible!'

'Exactly,' Llew said. 'Can we see your Rhodri now, please? Even if he has nothing to tell us, at least we'll have followed up that line of enquiry.'

Gareth went to the foot of the stairs.

'Rhodri!' he bawled. 'Can you hear me? Come down here, boyo, quick sharp! The police want a word with you!'

This was the summons that Rhodri had been dreading. He came slowly down the stairs, dressed in his shabby striped pyjamas and bunny slippers and looking far younger than his ten years.

The constable looked at Rhodri sternly. 'Now then, boyo, listen carefully. Your young friend has gone missing.'

'Has he?' Rhodri opened his eyes wide and Llew knew at once that the child was involved in Basil's disappearance.

'So, you know who I'm talking about, then!'

'Oh! Not really, but I expect it must be Basil if his parents are here?'

Cheeky young devil, thought Llew.

'What I want to know is, did you see anything of the boy when you went out to play after tea?'

'No, I didn't.'

'Are you quite sure about that?'

'He's already said he didn't!' Mrs Evans snapped, coming to the defence of her pet lamb.

'Please, Mrs Evans. Let me handle this. I want you to think very carefully, Rhodri. I believe you know more about this than you're letting on. Where was Basil when you saw him last?'

'Rhodri!' Gareth roared. 'Speak up this minute, boy, or do I have to take my belt to you?'

Rhodri burst into tears. He was no match for the two men. He knew they were going to wring it out of him sooner or later.

'He was at the Town Hall,' he

sobbed. 'That's all I know, honest!'

'That sounds right,' Ruth spoke up. 'When Basil asked if he could go out, he said he wanted to go and see the young people going into the dance. I thought at the time it seemed odd, but Basil gets funny ideas in his head sometimes. Perhaps he thought they'd all be wearing fancy dress. Anyway, there didn't seem any harm in letting him go, so long as he was home by eight o'clock. But then, when he didn't come, and he didn't come . . . ' She broke off, her poor face puckered with emotion.

Bob put his arm round her shaking shoulders and murmured something in her ear.

Llew Roberts turned back to Rhodri. 'Come now, Rhodri lad. You must know more than that. Did he go inside the hall? Was he still at the hall when you left? Was anyone else around at the time?'

Rhodri hung his head, not daring to look at Llew. But his eyes flew open when his father took him by the shoulders, shaking him none too gently.

'You're not telling the whole story, are you, lad? Better get if off your chest now, or it'll be all the worse for you later on. What were the two of you doing at the hall, eh? Up to no good, I'll be bound!'

Rubbing his eyes with his knuckles, Rhodri continued his tale.

'We heard they had pop and biscuits at the dance, Da. Basil thought we might be able to get some, see? So I bunked him in through the little window at the back. But then I heard somebody coming, and I had to run for it. I don't know what happened after that.'

'Leaving your mate to face the music!' Llew said scornfully.

'I did try to get in to see what was going on, but a lady stopped me at the door and sent me away. I didn't dare ask her if she'd seen Basil, because if he was hiding somewhere then she might find him and he'd be in trouble. That's all I know, honest!'

'Honest? You don't know the meaning of the word!' his father said in disgust. 'Get back up those stairs and we'll sort you out in the morning!'

Rhodri scuttled off, his mother following him, clucking like a hen.

'Can we get into the Town Hall at this time of night?' Bob asked. 'We've looked everywhere else we can think of. It's just possible that Basil did manage to hide somewhere inside, as the boy says.'

'We'll go and wake up Gwil Jones. He's the caretaker. He'll have a key.'

Llew Roberts led the way out of the Evans's front door, promising to come back the next day.

'Because there's more to this than meets the eye, Gareth man! That boy of yours knows more than he's letting on, and breaking into a public building is serious business, see? You should. straighten him out before he goes to the bad in a big way.'

The little party hurried silently

through the town, each with their own thoughts and with Ruth shaking inwardly, praying for Basil to be found alive.

Roused from his comfortable bed, Gwil Jones led the way to the Town Hall.

'I don't know what the world's coming to. Isn't it bad enough there's a war on, without such nonsense as this?'

As expected, the hall seemed deserted.

'Basil!' Ruth shouted. 'Basil! Are you here? Can you hear me?'

'Mummy!' A muffled voice reached them from far away, and Ruth caught her breath.

'Mummy!' There it was again.

'It's coming from the cupboard where they keep the ledgers and that!' Gwil shouted. 'Hang on, I'll get the key!'

There was an endless pause while he hurried off to the main office, and then he wrestled the door open while Ruth and Bob looked on in a fever of anticipation.

Basil looked up at them, blinking in the light. 'I thought nobody would come until Monday,' he sobbed.

Ruth reached out and gathered him into her arms. The post mortems could wait until later. For now, it was enough that her son was safe.

Marina Gets A Job

'How are things going with you and Emlyn?' Marina asked Marged, more out of politeness than because she really cared. She had to keep in with Marged if she wanted to maintain contact with Tim Parry!

'Oh, he's lovely!' Marged boasted. 'Taking me to the pictures this week, he is.' She failed to mention that Emlyn had been pestering her about Marina, asking if she thought there was any chance for him with her.

'She likes somebody else, I think,' Marged had answered truthfully. 'How would you like to go to the pictures with me, Emlyn? There's sure to be a good film coming on when the bill changes.'

'Might as well. There's nothing else to do around here,' he'd muttered.

That response was hardly what

Marged had hoped for, but as her mother was fond of saying, 'From little acorns, great oak trees grow.'

'Our Tim and Catrin Harris had a big row the other day,' she said now, to Marina.

'Really!' Marina was delighted to hear it. 'What was it about — do you know?'

'I could hardly miss knowing, could I, the way they were shouting at each other. In the parlour they were, and me in the kitchen, see? She wanted to know why he didn't ask her to dance at the hop the other night, and he said he had to look after you, because you're a visitor and he promised your mam.'

Marina giggled. 'I bet she didn't like that.'

'Well, she told him that she didn't care what he did, she wasn't interested — and our Tim said if that was the case, why did she bother coming all the way over to the house? After a bit she stormed out, slamming the door behind her. He didn't bother going after her,

180

which was probably what she was hoping for, so there you are.'

'They could make it up, though. I wish he'd ask me to go out with him. Do you think he might?'

'Maybe if I twist his arm.' Marged caught sight of her friend's face and knew she'd said the wrong thing. 'Oh, I didn't mean it like that, Marina! I was only thinking that he might be off women for a bit, if Catrin's thrown him over, see? How about arranging another foursome with Emlyn?'

'To do what, though? I don't want to go up the mountain again. I broke the strap on my sandals last time, scrambling over that rough ground.'

'I could ask Tim. I'm sure he'd come up with something. How would you fancy going down the pit, to see where he works?'

'Not on your life. You're not getting me going a mile underground in a tiny cage.'

'You could see the lovely pit ponies,' Marged said, grinning.

'No, thank you very much. And stop teasing. I believed you for a minute there!'

'How silly you are! Listen now, I think we should see if we can make you look a bit more grown-up than you do. Tim goes for the more sophisticated type. You're still a schoolgirl in his eyes. Very pretty, I'll grant you that, but a lot younger than Catrin Harris, in more ways than one.'

'I'm not a schoolgirl any more,' Marina insisted. 'Didn't I tell you I've finished with all that, never mind what my parents say. But Mum says that if they let me leave school then I've got to find a job, but I don't know where to start. It's not as if we're staying here for ever, is it? And who's going to employ me if they think I'll be throwing in the towel before they've got me trained?'

'Actually I'm in the same boat,' Marged sympathised. 'I left school a year ago, but Mam needed me at home for a while when she wasn't well. What I'd really like to do is to work at the telephone exchange. It's supposed to be a lot of fun. I happen to know that one of the girls is leaving to get married, so there's going to be a vacancy. Why don't we go and ask about it before they have a chance to advertise?'

'I'd have to ask Mum. She might not be very keen.'

'No. Try for the job first, and then you can go and tell her afterwards if you get it. If they turn you down, she'll be none the wiser.'

Marina hesitated. 'I don't know. We've just had a lot of trouble with my little brother and they're still on edge. There's been a lot of talk about people telling lies and keeping secrets. I don't want them thinking I can't be trusted.'

'Nonsense! It's not the same thing at all. Just say that I'm trying for a job and I want you to come with me for moral support. If you did get offered a job you could just go home and say you were in the right place at the right time.'

'What would we have to do at this telephone exchange, then?'

'You sit in front of a switchboard; people ring up to ask for a number and you put them through. Frances — that's the girl who's engaged to be married — told me they have such fun there. Sometimes they listen in to the conversations and they overhear all sorts of things.'

'Surely they're not supposed to do that?'

'Everybody knows you mustn't say anything confidential over the phone, so what difference does it make?'

Marina still wasn't sure about going for an interview. It was one thing to stop going to school, which she'd never enjoyed very much in any case, but quite another to step into the grown-up world of work.

'It would make Tim look at you differently if you worked at the telephone exchange,' Marged said slyly, 'and think what you could do with the money you earned!'

'I'd have to give it to Mum for my keep.'

'Not all of it, surely? She'd let you keep some for clothes and makeup.'

'Makeup! I can't see Dad agreeing to that!' Marina groaned, but the idea was beginning to take hold. 'All right, let's do it!'

★　★　★

Very few people in the town possessed a telephone of their own. There was one at the Town Hall and several at the colliery, and some of the bigger shops were also on the phone. Other than that, only the more important people qualified for one. They included the two doctors, the mine owner, the police and the clergy. Other people had to make do with one of the public call boxes, where they had to feed coins into a slot before the operator would put them through.

When you were successfully connected, you pressed Button A to continue the call and your money disappeared inside a locked container;

otherwise you pressed Button B to get your money returned. Children made a habit of nipping into the phone booths to see if anyone had forgotten to press Button B; it was surprising what you could buy with the proceeds.

'Yes, I suppose it's all right for you to go with Marged when she goes for her interview,' Ruth told Marina. 'It'll give you a chance to see how these things work before your own turn comes. Having an interview, I mean. Not that they'll let you into the room with her, I shouldn't think.'

'No, Mum.'

But just in case, Marina made sure she was as well turned out as possible. She polished her old school shoes and darned a hole in her ankle socks. She might look shabby, but she could at least be clean and tidy.

Nobody was more surprised than Marina when she was offered a job!

Marged had been accepted at once. The supervisor had known her for years and didn't even bother to talk about references or experience.

'I suppose you heard about Frances leaving? Well, this saves us the cost of advertising in the paper. When can you start?'

'Right away!' Marged had beamed.

'Good. We're really short-staffed. Another of my girls is engaged to an Air Force chap and she's determined to marry him as soon as possible, so she'll be off to live in England, just like Frances!'

That was when the supervisor turned to look at Marina and seemed to like what she saw.

'I don't suppose you want a job as well, do you?'

Marina was about to open her mouth to explain her circumstances, but Marged got in first.

'This is my friend, Marina Greene. She lives near us, up the Llandeilo Road.'

'Very well, Miss Greene; what do you think? Would you like to come and work here?'

Marina swallowed hard. 'Yes, please, I'd like to, very much!'

'Good! Then you're hired!'

* * *

Basil scuffed along with his eyes downcast, well aware that if his parents saw him he'd be yelled at and told to pick up his feet. But he didn't care. Nobody cared about what he wanted or what he thought! His only friend in the world was Mr Rees, the old miner. He would go and talk to him.

However, when Basil reached the allotment he was disappointed to find that his friend was nowhere to be seen. He decided to wait for a while to see if the man turned up. There was nothing else to do anyway.

He reached over to pull up a carrot.

'What's going on here, then?' Basil hadn't heard Emrys padding up behind him in his old plimsolls. He dropped the carrot as if it was burning hot.

'I didn't mean to steal, Mr Rees,

honestly!' he stammered.

'Did anyone say anything about stealing? I offered you a carrot the other day, so what's another one between friends?

'I heard about your bit of trouble the other night, boyo,' the old man went on, choosing his words with care. While he certainly didn't mind giving the child a carrot, he didn't want to give the impression that he condoned the taking of things that belonged to other people, no matter how small.

'How do you know about that, Mr Rees?'

'Oh, Gwil Jones is a pal of mine. At school together, we were, back in the dark ages. I met him in the tobacconist's just now, and he mentioned having a bit of excitement. Thought the Germans had landed, he did, when Llew Roberts come pounding at his door. Quite relieved, he was, when it was only because of a little lad locked in a cupboard where he had no business being in the first place.'

Basil's face turned the colour of his friend's beetroot.

'It was all a mistake,' he muttered.

'You can say that again! I suppose you had a thrashing when you got home? I hear Rhodri Evans won't be able to sit down for the next week or so.'

But Basil's parents hadn't lain a finger on him. When he'd reached home that night, carried on his father's shoulders, he'd been put to bed, soothed and petted by Ruth. His last thought as he'd drifted off to sleep had been that everything was going to be all right.

He had reckoned without Rhodri spilling the beans. The next morning both Bob and Ruth had read him the riot act.

'To think that any child of mine would even consider breaking into town property with the idea of stealing what was inside!' Bob thundered. 'The Greenes have always been as honest as the day is long. How has it come to this, I ask myself?'

'There wasn't anything there but a few rock cakes, Dad!'

Bob clenched his fists inside his trouser pockets. For two pins he'd let fly, but somehow he managed to control himself. The boy had to learn, but he was only a child, and had to be dealt with accordingly.

He had issued a little sermon about how it was wrong to steal, but it had been hard to tell if anything was truly sinking in.

Then it had been Ruth's turn. When Basil saw the tears rolling down his mother's face he had almost started to blubber himself. She was extremely disappointed in him, she'd said quaveringly.

'Can I go now?' he'd asked, when his mother seemed to have run out of words.

'No, you may not!' Bob had told him. 'We haven't decided on your punishment yet. For a start, I'm going to stop your pocket money for a month.'

'But, Dad! How am I going to get my *Beano*?'

'You should have thought of that before. Maybe doing without for a time will be the best thing for you.'

Basil had sloped off, feeling very hard done by.

Now he stood in Emrys Rees's allotment, his head drooping in shame.

'I didn't get a hiding but they won't let me see Rhodri any more,' he announced, aware that Mr Rees was expecting a reply to his question. 'And they've stopped my pocket money, so I won't be able to get the *Beano* or any sweets for weeks! It just isn't fair!'

'It sounds fair enough to me, *bach*. It's in the Bible, see. 'Thou shalt not steal'. If you do wrong, you have to take the punishment. That's the law, see, both God's and man's.'

Well, he'd said his piece. Maybe if the boy kept coming to see him at the allotment instead of getting in with bad companions, it might be a good thing. There wasn't much he could get up to there. Maybe he could help with the weeding and suchlike? It might make the lad feel better about himself if he had something useful to occupy him.

'Have you ever tried your hand at gardening, young Basil?' he asked him now.

'Dad won't let me touch the garden, Mr Rees. I tried weeding once, as a surprise, but he said I pulled up the young vegetable shoots by mistake. He said he didn't do all that digging and hoeing and planting to have me coming along behind him undoing all his good work.'

Emrys had to smile.

'There is a knack to gardening, true enough. I could teach you how to tell the difference, *bach*, if you'd like to try. My old back isn't what it used to be, see. I could use a helper now and then.'

In truth he was extremely fit for his age, and could have shown many a younger man a thing or two, but Basil wasn't to know that.

'All right, Mr Rees. I'll ask Mum if I

can come down each day and give you a hand.'

'That's right, *bach*. You tell your mam what you'll be getting up to and then she won't have to worry.' Then he told Basil to run along because the Town Hall clock had just struck twelve, and he'd be wanting his dinner.

Basil ran off happily. Mr Rees was his friend. Who needed Rhodri when they had Mr Rees?

An Exciting Night Out!

Ruth was feeling a lot more cheerful. After all her worries over the children, both of them now seemed to have settled down nicely.

Marina was happy in her new job, and in the excitement of it all she seemed to have forgotten all about her infatuation with the Parry boy. It had only been puppy love, of course, but even so, it had still been a worry to her parents.

As for Basil, he was happy working with Emrys Rees on his allotment. Ruth hadn't been sure about this at first, but when she'd spoken to Bessie about it, she'd received a glowing report of Emrys, whom the Parrys had known all their lives.

'He'll come to no harm with Emrys, Mrs Greene, take it from me. He'll be a good influence on the boy.'

Ruth had winced at that, but guessed that Bessie hadn't meant anything by it. Basil had come under the influence of that dreadful Rhodri and had behaved badly as a result, but he was just as much to blame in his own way.

Although her children seemed to be happy and settled, however, Ruth herself was beginning to fret under the dull routine which she had to endure day after day.

She said as much to her husband.

'You should get out more, love,' he told her.

'I do. I go down town and do my shopping, and I've taken out membership at the library. But none of that is very inspiring. Can't we do something together occasionally?'

'We go for walks together, don't we?'

'I mean, can't we go *out* together sometimes? The pictures or somewhere?'

'Can't be done, love. You know we can't both be out in the evening, leaving the boy by himself, and then there's

Mrs Thomas. She's the main reason we came down here in the first place. I tell you what, why don't you have a word with Bessie Parry? The girls are good friends now; why can't the two of you be the same?'

When Ruth made a tentative approach, Bessie was delighted.

'You can come down the chapel with me on Wednesday nights, Mrs Greene, to our ladies' group. We have speakers and classes and that. Some of it is very interesting, all about how to manage with the rations. We learned how to make a lovely fatless sponge last month. Not that it's as good as the cakes I used to make before the war, but then, nothing is the same as it was. Seven o'clock it starts. Shall I call for you at half-past six, then? We can walk down together.'

'You go along, love,' Bob said later, when Ruth told him about the ladies' group. 'Do you good to get out for a bit.'

Ruth was less than enchanted with

the idea but at least she'd have other adults to chat to, and she might make new friends.

As it happened, the first person she met was Eileen Evans, mother of the dreadful Rhodri. Despite everything, Ruth was prepared to greet Mrs Evans politely, if coolly, and she was annoyed when the woman literally stuck her nose in the air as she sailed past.

'Ignore her,' Bessie said comfortingly. 'She always was a bit touched!'

The speaker for the evening was a hearty woman in a green overall, and the subject of her talk was Make Do And Mend, which was one of the familiar slogans of the war. She displayed several items which, she said, they might like to copy.

One was a gingham dress for a little girl, which had undergone a startling transformation after being worn out by its owner, or possibly a succession of owners. The top half of the bodice had been replaced by a yoke and sleeves knitted in obviously recycled wool.

'It isn't new yarn, of course,' the presenter explained. 'The idea is that you unravel a worn pullover and use that.'

'It seems silly to me,' Mrs Evans argued. 'I mean, why use wool at all? Why not bits of material from some other old frock?'

'Certainly you could do that, madam. This is only meant to start you thinking by demonstrating what is possible. Now I want to explain how you can turn your summer frocks to give them a new lease of life.'

'Oh, I wouldn't dream of wearing an old frock inside out!' Mrs Evans complained, causing Ruth to raise her eyes to the ceiling.

Someone in the audience tittered, but the presenter soldiered on.

'The idea here is to unpick all the seams and then sew the dress up again, so that the faded pattern is now on the inside. With a bit of rick-rack braid added, or some different buttons, it could be made very smart indeed.'

Ruth rather liked the idea. She had a favourite dress that she'd owned since she was first married, but it was sadly faded now and she'd been on the point of cutting it up for dusters.

'The trouble is,' she told Bessie in an undertone, 'I'd have to sew it by hand, and the seams might give way at some inopportune moment.'

'No need for that,' Bessie whispered back. 'You can have a loan of my old treadle. Come round to the house any time, and I'll show you how to thread it up.'

'Thanks!' Ruth whispered back.

While tea was being served, several of the other women came over to be introduced to Ruth. One wanted to sign her up for Red Cross meetings, while another wondered if she could sing soprano, as they were trying to recruit new members for the choir.

Ruth regretfully declined the offer to join the choir. She enjoyed warbling away as much as the next woman, but she knew she would let the side down if they ever got her in a choir robe. The Welsh were famous for their voices and she'd heard some magnificent singing coming from the Methodist Chapel on Sunday mornings. The beauty and the power of their music reached as far as the bedroom over the shop where the Greenes were having a lie-in.

'Enjoy the evening, did you?' Bessie asked her as they were walking home.

'I thought that idea of knitting door mats out of old stockings was quite good,' Ruth answered diplomatically. 'I might try that when we go back to Hemel. I've a good few in a bag at home, all too far gone to mend, I'm afraid.'

'You should cobble them up if you can. At least they'd give you a bit of warmth on your legs, not like colouring them with gravy browning like some women do.'

'You haven't seen these old stockings of mine, Mrs Parry. They're more ladder than leg, if you get my meaning.'

Bessie sighed. 'Ah, well, you can but try.'

'I say, what on earth was the matter with that woman, treating me like a bad smell under her nose?'

'Eileen? I told you, she isn't quite sixteen ounces to the pound. It's this business with the boys, of course. She's embarrassed, and I would be, too, if any of mine behaved the way Rhodri does. It's not just childish mischief he gets up to. It's downright devilment. If they don't take him in hand soon, he'll be in real trouble before he's much older. And a word to the wise, Mrs Greene — make sure he stays away from your Basil.'

'Oh, don't worry. We've already impressed on Basil that he's to have nothing more to do with Rhodri.'

'That isn't quite what I meant, Mrs Greene. There's a mean streak in that boy, and it showed itself when he was very small. I used to be a teacher in the Sunday School, see, looking after the little ones, and Rhodri wasn't just a handful, he was — well, I don't know how to put it. Wicked is too strong a word to use for a Christian child, but I thought that about him, even then.'

Ruth was inclined to dismiss this as a bit much. Bessie was a staunch member of the chapel, and Methodists were well known for their strict moral code.

Ruth prided herself on being honest and truthful, and she was trying to bring up her children to have similar values, but she didn't think of herself as being overly strict.

Still, both sets of beliefs were no doubt good in their own way, she thought. They could exist perfectly well side by side.

'You remember what I'm telling you, Mrs Greene,' Bessie remarked, her expression serious. 'I wouldn't trust that boy further than I could throw him, and that's a fact.'

'You surely don't mean that he'd try to hurt Basil?' Ruth was incredulous.

'I don't say he'd do your boy any physical harm,' Bessie countered, but would say no more.

Dreadful News!

Marina loved her job and quickly learned what was expected of her. The only thing she disliked about it was the clothing she was expected to wear — a horrid black dress with a removable white collar and cuffs.

'It's what most women have to wear when they go out to work,' Ruth explained. 'In shops, offices, even in restaurants. It's very practical, really. Black doesn't show the dirt and the white bits are easy enough to wash and dry overnight. Think yourself lucky that your uniform was provided for you. Buying a dress would set you back eight clothing coupons.'

'But it's second hand!' Marina wrinkled her nose. 'And it must have been made for some bigger person. See how it hangs on me? And why do we have to dress this way when nobody ever sees us? I'd rather wear trousers like a land girl, or dungarees like women in factories have to do.'

'Perish the thought!' Bob had been passing through the kitchen and heard the tail end of this conversation. 'No daughter of mine is going to wear trousers! You don't want to get a reputation for being fast.'

'I don't see why, Dad! Girls wear tennis shorts, and jodhpurs for riding, so what's the difference?'

'Personally I think we women *should* be able to wear trousers,' Ruth announced. 'Stockings are hard to come by, and you men in your trousers have no idea what it's like to wear a skirt in winter! I'd like to make you all wear a kilt for a day or two and see what you thought about women in trousers then!'

Bob ignored her. When this beastly war was over, women would give up working on the land and in factories. They'd go back to being housewives, and never don trousers again.

As it was, his daughter was looking far too grown up these days for a girl not yet seventeen. He couldn't put his finger on what had made the difference; possibly it was the hairstyle. There was a big difference between wearing your hair in plaits and putting it up in a roll, as the girl was doing now.

He said something to that effect, but she looked him straight in the eye and said that working in the telephone exchange was like the army; your hair wasn't allowed to touch your collar.

★ ★ ★

'Have you heard any juicy conversations yet?' Marged asked Marina when she finally had a chance to catch up with her friend. They were on different shifts and rarely had a chance to speak to each other.

'No, I haven't. It's not very nice to eavesdrop on people's private chats.'

'Oh, listen to her! Telephone calls are like postcards. If you don't want people

206

to know your business then you should write a letter and seal it. Don't be so hoity-toity, Marina!'

But Marina thought that listening in was like reading someone's diary.

However, all her good intentions were to fall by the wayside when she put through a trunk call to the doctor's wife.

'I'm putting you through now, caller,' she said, in her most professional voice, waiting until the other party came on the line; occasionally something went wrong and crossed wires resulted in a mix-up.

'Hello, Mum! Can you hear me? I'm calling to say that I've got a few days off from the hospital and I'll be home on Friday, all right?'

Marina was about to pull out the plug when her attention was attracted by what the girl said next.

'Do you know those new people at the shop?'

'I know who you mean, dear, but I never go in there. We're registered at the Home and Colonial. Why do you ask?'

It would have taken a stronger person than Marina to tune out at that moment. She felt she had to know what was being said in case it was something about her family. She almost stopped breathing in her effort not to be discovered.

'Oh, it's just that they're related to the Thomas family, aren't they?'

'I believe so. I seem to recall that the woman is Dora Thomas's sister.'

'Well, one of the nurses in my set has a brother in the Navy, and she's been terribly upset because his ship was torpedoed and she didn't know if he was all right. Anyhow, she had good news this morning when he phoned to let her know that he was safe. She was on duty with me at the time, and Sister actually let her take the call, the circumstances being what they were. Joan has mentioned me in her letters to him, so he knows where I'm from, and he told her that Idris Thomas was on his ship, but was lost when it sank. Sad, isn't it? Oh, dash it — is that the pips already? And I'm out of change. See you on Friday, Mum.'

Idris! It was all Marina could do to stop herself from breaking into the conversation to demand to be told more. In a panic she rushed to her supervisor.

'I've had bad news,' she gasped. 'I'm just going to pop home, all right?'

'You're not, you know!' The woman snorted. 'People are depending on you. Don't you know there's a war on? You'll stay at your post until your shift is up, Miss Greene. Pop home indeed! I've never heard such a thing!'

So Marina had to stay where she was, which was highly unnecessary because few other calls came in that afternoon.

★   ★   ★

It was also a quiet afternoon in the shop. Bob Greene was sitting on a high stool behind the counter, reading some government directive which had come in the post. Mamgu was seated nearby, hoping that one of her cronies would drop in for a chat.

'I could do with a cup of tea,' she remarked, just as the very same thought was going through Bob's head.

'I'll go and make one, shall I? I'll be back shortly, Mrs Thomas.'

But at that moment the doorbell jangled, and Bob turned back to the counter, ready to serve the customer. He froze when he saw that the new arrival was a fresh-faced boy, delivering one of the dreaded telegrams from the War Office.

'Telegram for Thomas,' he piped up.

Mamgu's face turned white. 'Not my Dai!' she moaned.

Bob accepted the envelope in a shaking hand. Neither of them noticed that the boy had left, letting the door swing to behind him.

'Do you want me to open this, Mrs Thomas? I mean, it's not addressed to me, but there's nobody else here.' Bob knew he was babbling but he really didn't want to break bad news to her. What if she had another stroke on the spot? Where on earth was Ruth? There should be another woman here at a time like this.

The old lady was looking at him now, with such misery in her eyes that he thought it best not to keep her in suspense any longer.

Using his penknife he slit the telegram open.

'We regret to inform you . . . enemy action . . . It's Idris, Mrs Thomas. I'm afraid his ship has been sunk.'

'Dead, then, is he?' she quavered.

'It says missing, presumed drowned. I'm so sorry, Mrs Thomas.'

She began to rock back and forth, keening softly.

Bob slipped into the kitchen. That cup of tea was needed more than ever now. He wondered if he should put a drop of something into Mrs Thomas's cup. He understood that she had signed the pledge years ago, but did that include lacing a hot drink for medicinal purposes? According to her, strong drink was the devil's tool, and he didn't want to be accused of starting her on the downward path.

What else could he do, then? Reaching for a little bottle which Ruth kept on the mantelpiece, he shook two aspirin tablets into his hand.

Ground up in the tea they should take the edge off her pain.

When he went back into the shop, she was still rocking back and forth, with her apron over her head, but she stopped when he offered her the cup and began to drink the tea quite sensibly.

The doorbell jangled again. This time it was a tall, balding man who was not one of their regular customers. He looked none too pleased and Bob wondered what was up. He wasn't left wondering for long.

'Are you Greene?'

'Yes, that's right. Can I help you?'

'I certainly hope so. It's about the

vegetables you sent round. I think you've been overcharging your customers and I want to know what you mean to do about it.'

Bob frowned. 'I don't understand. We don't sell vegetables. I just grow them for our own use, as do most people nowadays.'

'That wasn't what your boy told me when he brought them to the door.'

'My boy? Oh, I don't think so . . . '

'Well, he gave his name as Basil Greene!'

★   ★   ★

Ruth was faced with the unenviable task of breaking the news of Idris's loss to poor Dora. 'Better make sure you put the ward sister in the picture before you say anything,' Bob counselled. 'It's bound to come as a terrible shock and Dora may need a sedative or something. I only wish we had some sort of knock-out drops to give Mrs Thomas, but she's insistent that she doesn't want anything.'

'Can't you come with me?' Ruth begged. 'Surely it won't hurt to close the shop for once. You can put a notice on the door, explaining that there's been a bereavement.'

'Sorry, love; you'll have to manage on your own. I have something important to do while you're gone.'

Ruth was so distraught at the thought of what lay ahead of her that she didn't ask what could possibly be more important than the loss of poor Dora's son. Instead, she made her way to the cottage hospital feeling quite sick with dread.

Dora received the news with dangerous calm. 'I always knew something like this would happen. I begged him not to join the Navy. Isn't it enough that I have to worry about your father being at sea, I told him, but would be listen to me? I might as well have been talking to the wall.'

There was silence for a while, and then she asked, 'Do you think they'll let us bury him in Bedwen? I'd at least like to have a grave to visit. Idris wouldn't seem so far away then.'

Ruth gulped. Hadn't Dora taken in what the telegram said?

'It said, 'missing, presumed drowned',' Ruth murmured.

'Oh, yes, of course. 'Full fathom five my father lies.' Remember doing that in school, Ruth? Was that Shakespeare or Dickens?'

'Shakespeare, I think. The Tempest.'

Ruth knew very well where the quotation was from. She remembered learning the words because she'd thought them so beautiful and mysterious.

'*Full fathom five my father lies;*
Of his bones are coral made:
Those are pearls that were his eyes . . . '

She would never think them beautiful again, and she certainly wasn't going to finish the quotation for Dora.

'Of course, they wouldn't bring him home, even if he'd died on a battlefield,' Dora said, nodding. 'They don't, do they? They bury people over there.'

She sounded so reasonable that Ruth was frightened. It was shock, of course. Should she call Sister? But that good woman was already on her way, bearing a hypodermic syringe in an enamelled dish.

'Doctor wants you to have this, Mrs Thomas,' she said kindly, rolling up the sleeve of Dora's nightgown.

It was as if the prick of the needle punctured Dora's composure as well as her skin, for suddenly she began to weep, hard, wrenching sobs that shook her whole body.

'Where is Dai?' she cried. 'Is he coming? I want Dai! I want Dai!'

Aware of alarmed stares from the other patients, Sister beckoned to a hovering probationer. 'Fetch some screens and put them around this bed, Nurse. Quickly, now! Don't stand there gawping like an idiot.'

'What should I do?' Ruth asked, worried. 'Would it be best if I left now?'

'You stay with Mrs Thomas until she falls asleep,' Sister directed. 'She may not respond to you, but it will be a comfort if she knows that you're with her. We'll take over after that. Sad to say, I'm afraid this isn't the first time one of my patients has had such bad news. In a day or two, I'll ask Mrs Matthews to have a word. She lost one of her own sons who was fighting in Africa. She'll know just how your cousin is feeling.'

Waiting for the bus which would take her home, Ruth wondered whether Dai Thomas might be given compassionate leave to spend time with his wife. Probably not. Did he even know that Idris was gone? The War Office must have the lad's home address, which was why the telegram had come to the shop, but nobody would have thought of notifying Dai. Perhaps she ought to get in touch with him; but how? He was off on the ocean somewhere, doing the dangerous job of ferrying vital supplies to Britain and assisting with troop movement to other countries. At least, she supposed he was. Civilians weren't supposed to know what was going on.

'Mum!' Ruth got off the bus and looked around to see her daughter hurrying towards her. 'Have you heard the news? Isn't it dreadful? I wanted to come home to be with you all, but I wasn't allowed.'

'Poor Idris, you mean? We had a telegram. I've just come back from breaking the news to Auntie Dora.'

'How awful for you! How did she take it?'

'She was very distressed. She broke down in the end and Sister had to give her something. Even so, I doubt it's really sunk in yet. I'll have to go back in a day or two, and I'm not looking forward to it one bit.'

'You look a bit shaky yourself, Mum. Why don't we pop into that little tea-room and see if they've got anything worth eating?'

'Yes, why not? I could do with something before I face them at home.'

'Oh, you mean Mamgu! She's bound to be terribly upset too.'

'Yes, and she seems convinced that Idris's father will be next on the casualty list. It's no good telling her that it won't happen because in his line of work I'm afraid it's all too likely.'

'I hate this war!' blurted out Marina.

Ruth reflected that the same sentiment was probably being voiced all around the world at that moment. Why, oh, why did men like Hitler and Mussolini, and that Japanese emperor, have to be so hungry for power, sweeping all before them? Surely they couldn't all be as mad as hatters, but she could think of no sane explanation for their actions.

★   ★   ★

Back at home, Bob had been waiting for Basil to come in from school. He was about to have an interview with that young man, which neither of them would enjoy.

What on earth had possessed the child to do such a wicked thing, especially so soon after that other episode on the night of the dance.

Bob's visitor to the shop that afternoon had been a Mr Russell, a retired schoolmaster who lived in a quiet road on the other side of the town. He had opened his door earlier that day to a boy who had an assortment of very fine vegetables in a trek cart.

'One of those two-wheeled jobs that Boy Scouts use for carrying their equipment,' he'd explained, in case Bob didn't understand what he was talking about. 'I had no quarrel with the vegetables themselves; very fine speci-mens they were indeed. But the prices seemed greatly inflated. I have my own garden, so I didn't want any, but I have two elderly maiden ladies living next door and they rely on me to keep an eye on anyone 'knocking around', as they say.'

'And this boy gave his name as Basil Greene?'

'Oh, yes. He spoke up quite readily

when I asked, 'And who is your father and what does he do?' and he said that you own this shop. So, as you see, here I am, and I'd like an explanation!'

'There's something not right here, Mr Russell. To start with, this isn't my shop. I'm simply running it for my wife's cousin while she's in hospital. And yes, my son is called Basil Greene, but he has no authority to sell the vegetables I grow. Furthermore, when I last looked outside, there were none missing! All I can say, Mr Russell, is that I shall look into this and report my findings to you later.'

Bob underwent a great deal of heart-searching while waiting for Basil to come home. He would have dismissed the story as nonsense had it not been for the fact that Russell had been given Basil's name. But why on earth would the child have been hawking food produce from door to door? Was it some scheme to make a bit of pocket money, to replace what was being withheld from him as punishment

221

for the Town Hall caper? Had he somehow purchased them wholesale, as it were, and then had to charge exorbitant rates in order to make a profit?

The back door banged, and Basil came racing in. 'Dad, Dad, something awful's happened!'

Bob sighed. He'd intended to keep the news of Idris's death a secret until this other business was cleared up, but probably the news was all around the town now and the boy had heard it from one of his new classmates.

'Yes, it's very sad, Basil. You must be very kind to Mamgu now.'

'Why? Has something happened to her?'

'I'm talking about the sad news we've had, about Auntie Dora's son, Idris, being killed at the war. Isn't that what you're talking about?'

'No, Dad. I didn't know. Was his ship blown up or what?'

Bob prayed for patience. Basil had never met his cousin, and at his age he was far too young to understand the tragic consequences of war.

'Come and sit down, old chap, and I'll tell you what we think happened.'

This topic dispensed with for the time being, Bob thought it wise to get down to business before the mood was broken.

'Now, what was your news, then, Basil? Something awful, you said?'

'Yes, Dad! Poor Mr Rees! Somebody went to his allotment in the night and stole all his vegetables! I thought he was going to have a fit!'

More Trouble For Basil

Emrys Rees felt as though all the stuffing had been knocked out of him. When he'd turned up at his allotment that morning, he hadn't intended to actually do any work. After he and young Basil had attended to the patch the evening before, there hadn't been a weed left in sight and the two of them had gloated over the rows of ripening vegetables.

But now, Emrys couldn't believe his eyes as he sat on his upturned pail, too disheartened even to light up his pipe.

He'd been counting on those vegetables to see him through the coming winter. A chap had to do something to keep body and soul together, especially now, when rationing could only be stretched to a little more than a shilling's worth of meat to do the whole week. That might amount to a single pork chop and three or four sausages, and heaven only knew what they put in sausages nowadays. Mostly bread and sage, probably.

But that was only part of what was distressing Emrys. Ever since his dear wife had died, he had used his work at the allotment as a way to handle his grief. All the digging and hoeing had brought a kind of peace.

Now that had been taken away from him, too.

He got up stiffly and wandered around, looking at other people's plots.

Brinley Harris had some fine cauliflowers coming along, and little Miss Rice had some very nice heads of cabbage. Nobody else had suffered any loss. The vandals had confined their activities to his garden alone.

Who could have done this? At first glance, seeing the wreckage, he had suspected some animal, but no, that couldn't be it. Dogs might have dug holes, and he'd occasionally had rabbits going for his lettuce and carrots, but this had the hallmark of human hands. The carrots and parsnips had been pulled up systematically and his curly kale seemed to have been chopped off with a knife.

It was too late in the season to replant now. Anger surged through his body. Why should this have happened to him? He'd always done his best to treat others as he'd have wanted to be treated himself, and so far as he knew, he didn't have an enemy in the world.

As a rule, Bedwen was a law-abiding place. But Emrys read the newspapers, of course, and he knew that there were bad apples who turned the upheaval of war to their own advantage. War profiteering was illegal but not unknown; most goods could be obtained on the black market.

Should he report his loss to the police? There was probably not much point. They could hardly conduct a house-to-house search looking for surplus produce. He smiled grimly at the very idea.

He might question his fellow gardeners when they turned up later; somebody might have seen something.

So he remained sitting on his upturned pail, sunk in thought, too dispirited to make a start on clearing up the mess. Neither did he make a move to go home. There was nothing for him there.

When Basil had arrived after school, it had been evident from his reaction that the chaos was just as much a shock to the boy as it had been to him, and Emrys had chided himself for having wondered, just for a brief moment, if the child might have been responsible for the disaster.

'What happened, Mr Rees? Everything looked so lovely yesterday, and now look at it! It's all spoiled.'

'I don't know, *bach*. It was this way when I turned up this morning, see?'

'But why would anybody do this? I don't understand.'

Emrys had no answer to this.

'Whoever it was doesn't know much

about gardening,' Basil went on, reaching down to pick up the green potato foliage. 'You said the spuds weren't ready to harvest yet. Give them another week or two, you said. Shall I give you a hand clearing up, Mr Rees? Perhaps it won't look so bad if I dig it over a bit.'

'No, no, *bach*. You go on home now.'

Basil ran home feeling highly indignant on his friend's behalf. All set to blurt out the story, he was shocked when his father broke the news of his cousin's death. Unfortunately, lots of people did die in the war and Basil had never met Cousin Idris. Of course, he felt saddened in a general sort of way, but he had no sense of a personal loss.

Finally Bob stopped going on about Idris and asked his son what it was that he'd been about to say. Basil needed no second bidding.

'Oh, Dad, it's so awful I can't believe it! Somebody has gone to Mr Rees's allotment and stolen all his stuff! All his lovely carrots and onions and potatoes and . . . '

'Never mind reciting the garden catalogue to me, son. Just tell me what happened.'

'I told you, Dad! I went there on the way home from school, to see if any weeds had come up in the night, cos that's my job now — Mr Rees shows me what the weeds look like, and then I pull them up. But when I got there, Mr Rees was just sitting about, looking sad. He said somebody must have come when the place was deserted and taken all his vegetables away. Isn't that the meanest thing you ever heard, Dad?'

'Yes, yes, Basil. Now, keep quiet for a minute and let me have a think.'

Like Emrys Rees, Bob now felt ashamed of himself for having suspected Basil of any wrong-doing. He knew his son well, and could always tell when he was keeping something from him. It would have taken a better actor than Basil to play the innocent after pulling a stunt like that. He decided to take the boy into his confidence.

'Something very strange happened

today,' he began.

'Yes, Dad?'

'A gentleman came to see me. His name is Mr Russell, and he lives on the other side of the town. Apparently a boy called at his house offering to sell him vegetables. Mr Russell became suspicious when the asking price was much too high. It was as if the boy had no idea how much to charge.'

'Cor! I bet he's the one who stole from Mr Rees!'

'Possibly.'

'But, Dad! Why did the man come to see *you*?'

'Well, lad, Mr Russell came here because, when asked to give his name, the boy said it was Basil Greene.'

Basil's eyes opened wide. 'Then he's a big fat fibber. It wasn't me who stole the veggies and tried to sell them! You do believe me, don't you, Dad?'

'Yes, Basil, I believe you. The thing we have to work out now is, who was that boy?'

'Rhodri, Dad! I bet it was Rhodri!'

* * *

Their first port of call was Mr Russell's house. Fortunately he was at home when they arrived.

'Ah, Mr Greene! Good of you to report back so promptly!'

'I won't beat about the bush, Mr Russell. This is my son, Basil. Is this the boy who attempted to sell vegetables to you early this morning?'

'No, it is not.'

'Are you quite sure about that?'

'Of course I'm sure, man! I'm hardly in my dotage yet!'

'Then would you mind coming along with us? We have a good idea of what's going on here, and we'd like you to take a look at the boy who I think might be the culprit.'

Eileen Evans was furious when she opened her door to the trio.

'Not you again! I thought we'd seen the back of you, I did.'

'We'd like a word with Rhodri, please. Is he here?'

231

'No, he's gone out with his father, up to the Rec.'

At that moment, Gareth and Rhodri came round the side of the house; Rhodri carrying a football and looking cheerful and carefree. But his expression changed when he saw the visitors. His gaze travelled from Bob to Mr Russell, and then he bolted. His father caught him by the collar and hauled him back.

'Now what's he done?' Gareth Evans demanded, as he struggled to control his squirming son.

'Is this the boy, Mr Russell?' Bob asked.

'Yes, it is,' came the firm reply.

'Then, Mr Evans, I'd like Rhodri to explain why he has been trying to hawk stolen goods around the town, giving his name as Basil Greene!'

There was a gasp from Mrs Evans before she slid gracefully to the ground.

★ ★ ★

After a time, life settled back down for the Greene family. Their feelings of sadness over Idris were still raw, and they would continue to mourn, but life had to go on. Like many other families, they just had to get on with it.

Mamgu derived some comfort from the fact that at long last she'd received a letter from her son, Dai. It was impossible to tell where it had been posted, and much of its contents had been blacked out by the censor's pen, but it meant the world to her.

Dai had handled that same flimsy paper, which she folded and unfolded twenty times a day, and at night she slept with the letter under her pillow.

'Poor old girl,' Bob confided to Ruth. 'It's hard losing a grandson at her age.'

'It's hard at any age,' his wife retorted.

Ruth was still smarting from the awful blunder that she'd made when visiting Dora that day. The poor thing had been saying over and over again how much she missed Idris.

'You don't know what it's like, losing a child.'

'Oh, I'm sure I do! I was desperate when Basil went missing.'

When Dora's eyes flashed, Ruth knew she'd put her foot in it.

'Really, Ruth! There's no comparison, no comparison whatsoever. Your Basil spent the night locked in a cupboard. My Idris is dead and gone!'

'But at the time I really believed that something must have happened to Basil, that's all I meant,' Ruth stammered, but Dora was in a huff and wasn't prepared to listen.

As for Basil, he felt disillusioned and betrayed, and he said as much to his father.

'Why did Rhodri want to get me into trouble like that, Dad? It was really, really beastly.'

'According to what Rhodri told his father, he didn't set out to frame you, lad. It was only when Mr Russell demanded to know who he was, that he blurted out your name because he was afraid of getting caught.'

'If you believe that, you'll believe anything,' Basil retorted, quoting his sister whose favourite saying this was at the moment.

'Don't be cheeky!' Bob frowned, but he was inclined to agree with Basil that Rhodri had planned the whole business with malice aforethought.

'What will happen to Rhodri now, Dad?'

'Don't ask me. It'll be up to Mr Rees if he wants to press charges.'

'Poor Mr Rees, though. He needed those veggies for the winter. Can't we give him some of ours? There's enough in that garden to sink a battleship.'

Thanking his lucky stars that Mamgu wasn't in the room to hear this unfortunate remark, Bob agreed that, if Basil would lend a hand with the weeding, they might be able to help Emrys out.

★   ★   ★

Marina was perhaps more affected by her cousin's death than her parents were. Being romantically inclined, she thought of Idris as a sort of Sir Lancelot — young and pure, a knight in shining armour, who'd died for his country. She also now understood for the first time that in times of war nobody's survival was certain. That meant that you had to squeeze all the enjoyment out of life that you could, while you had the chance.

She'd been waiting patiently for Tim Parry to invite her out, but it hadn't happened. Dare she precipitate matters?

Printed in one of Ruth's women's magazines there had been a letter written to the 'agony aunt' on just this subject. The writer had explained that she liked a certain young man at her place of work and she was sure the feeling was reciprocated. However, he seemed too shy to ask her out. Would it be all right for her to do the asking?

'No,' Aunt Anne had replied. 'It does not do to appear too forward. Gentlemen prefer to be the ones to make the first move. If he really likes you then he will pluck up the courage to ask you out. Why not make up a party of your friends to go rambling or cycling, and invite him to be part of the expedition? He will not feel threatened and then, in a more relaxed atmosphere than the office provides, you can get to know each other better.'

'Good grief!' Marina thought. 'She's Victorian — even though Queen Victoria's dead!'

And anyway, they had already done the group thing. What was the worst that could happen if she asked Tim for a date? It would be mortifying if he said no, but she decided to risk it.

An old film, 'Jesse James', was coming to the cinema. Tim enjoyed action movies, and this one, about the famous American outlaw, should be just his thing. It had been released in 1939, so it wasn't new, but there was no harm in that. She would have preferred something musical and romantic, but she supposed she could sit through this so long as Tim was by her side. She wasn't sure if he liked Henry Fonda, but Tyrone Power, who portrayed Jesse, was certainly a dreamboat. She had his picture, cut from a film magazine, in her scrapbook back in Hemel.

''Jesse James'? Might be worth seeing,' Tim mused. 'Are you offering to pay for me, Marina?'

'I thought we'd go dutch,' she said firmly. If he wasn't gentleman enough to pay for her ticket then she certainly wasn't going to waste her hard-earned cash on him. There was a limit!

She might share her sweet ration with him, though. Not chocolate, but toffees in a bag. She imagined leaning close to him to offer the bag, their hands touching as they both reached inside for a sweet.

⋆　⋆　⋆

Marina was delighted when, as they reached the cinema on the appointed evening, she caught sight of Catrin Harris standing in the queue with her friend, Gwyneth.

When Catrin noticed Tim she sent a furious glare in his direction.

'If looks could kill!' Marina thought, smothering a giggle. She whispered something to Tim, forcing him to incline his head towards her in order to hear what was being said. Just let Catrin conclude that they were being all lovey-dovey, thought Marina, as she simpered up at Tim.

The film wasn't bad. Marina wondered if the real Jesse James had been as handsome and daring as he was portrayed, or was he just a criminal who had preyed on the innocent? She'd always thought that the Wild West must have been a romantic place, but it might not have been so wonderful in real life.

On their way out of the cinema, they came face to face with Catrin and her friend. Marina immediately tucked her arm into Tim's and he did nothing to shake her off. Tim nodded to Catrin and didn't seem to mind when she tossed her head and deliberately turned her back on him.

Now came the exciting part! Walking home in the gloom, Marina had the perfect excuse for clinging to Tim. With no street lamps on, it was hard to see where you were going and she stumbled on purpose, giving a little squeal as she fell against him. With this encouragement he bent down and grazed her cheek with a gentle kiss.

'Oh, I did enjoy this evening,' she murmured. 'I really like a good film, don't you? I hope we can do it again sometime.'

'Might as well,' he told her.

She reached home in a daze of delight, which was heightened when he kissed her again, this time on the lips in a lingering fashion.

It took her a long time to get to sleep that night, with the result that she made mistakes at work the next day. She accidentally cut off an important trunk call which led to a demand from an irate customer to speak to her supervisor but Marina didn't care. She was in love, and she felt as if she were floating on air.

For his part, Tim had mixed feelings. He still loved Catrin, but she had to be brought to heel. No man wanted a wife who insisted on having her own way. Her place was to consider him in all things. When the time came for him to marry, Tim wanted a wife like his mother, who spent all her life catering to Len Parry's whims and was glad to do so.

It was good that Catrin was jealous. If she saw enough of him with Marina Greene, then she'd cave in and apologise for treating him in such an off-hand manner.

But Tim didn't feel that he was just using Marina. Oh, no, there was more to it than that. She had grown up a lot in the past few weeks and she was a very pretty girl. Then, too, her English ways had a novelty about them and he felt that he'd like to get to know her better.

Bessie Parry didn't suspect a thing. She believed her son was just being kind to the little visitor at the shop.

The misunderstanding between Tim and Catrin would iron itself out in time. Where there was true love, these things usually worked themselves out in the end.

Marged was the only one who saw through Tim.

'See you don't push Catrin too far or you'll lose her for good,' she warned.

'See if I care,' he countered.

'And mind you don't hurt Marina, either,' she snapped. 'She's my friend, see?'

★   ★   ★

'Good morning, Mr Thomas. I'm Lorna.' Bob looked round from the tins he was stacking on the shelves.

'Oh, good morning, er, Laura. Can I help you?'

'It's Lorna. I've come about Idris, Mr Thomas.'

Bob suddenly realised what she'd said. 'No, no, I'm not Mr Thomas. The name is Greene. I'm working here temporarily.'

'Oh, I see. Then where can I find Mr Thomas, please? Or his wife, if that's not possible.'

'Mr Thomas is away on active duty, and I'm afraid that his wife is in hospital. Would you like to tell me what this is about? Possibly I can be of assistance.'

Tears gathered in the girl's pale blue eyes. She really was a very pretty young woman, he noticed. Her light brown hair was gathered into the sort of arrangement that his own wife and daughter wore, and her clothing — although shabby now — had once been good. The coat and skirt fitted her slender figure to perfection.

'I'm Idris's fiancée,' she said quietly.

'I didn't know anything about what had happened until I read the casualty lists in the paper. I came as soon as I could, Mr Greene.'

'Oh, dear. I really don't know what to say. I'm sorry for your loss, of course, but beyond that . . . '

'Do you mind if I sit down, Mr Greene? I don't feel very well.'

'Of course. Of course. Do forgive me, Miss — er — Lorna. I was caught on the hop. I don't think we knew that Idris was engaged, you see.'

The girl sank down on to the wooden chair which was kept for customers to use while their orders were made up. She did look a bit wan. Bob hoped she wasn't going to faint.

'Look, you stay here. I think I'd better fetch my wife.'

He dashed into the kitchen, leaving the door ajar. He hoped this wasn't some ploy to shoplift. After Basil's experience with Rhodri, Bob had become cynical. If a mere child could be so Machiavellian, goodness knows what a grown woman might do.

Ruth had just placed some sour milk in a cloth and was in the act of hanging the bundle over a basin to drip. By the look of it she was making cottage cheese. Before the war she would have poured the milk down the drain, but they couldn't afford to waste it nowadays.

'Can you come?' he hissed. 'There's a girl out there who says she's Idris's financée.'

'What are you whispering for? Speak up, do. I can't make out a word you're saying.'

'Just come, all right?' he urged.

Ruth knew what to do at once. She took the girl into the kitchen, where the kettle was boiling merrily. She could at least offer her a cup of tea, the universal remedy for problems of all kinds.

What on earth would they do if the supply ships could no longer get through, and tea disappeared from the shops as so many things had already done?

'So, you're Idris's young lady, my husband tells me.'

'Yes, that's right. We were going to be married on his next leave, but now . . . ' She broke down and began to sob noisily.

'I'm so sorry.'

There was little more that Ruth could say. All across Britain, and throughout the empire, similar scenes were being enacted as wives and mothers, sisters and sweethearts, had to face the fact that they would never see their loved one again.

Not that the knowledge of this did anything to soothe the individual sufferer, such as this poor girl.

'And I've come all this way to see his family, but your husband tells me that there's nobody here belonging to Idris!'

'Actually, his grandmother is here, Mrs Thomas senior, but she isn't very well.'

Lorna's face brightened at once.

'Then can I speak to her?'

'Perhaps in a little while. She's sleeping just now. As I said, she's rather frail. You mentioned having come a long way. Where are you from?'

'Portsmouth.'

'Oh, that *is* a long way.'

Ruth was thinking fast. They couldn't let this girl travel back to Portsmouth today — she would have to stay the night; but where on earth were they to put her? The house was full to bursting as it was.

And would Dora want to see the girl?

Perhaps she would, as a last link with Idris. That would mean keeping Lorna under this roof for a longer period.

And how were they to feed her? Would it be crass to demand her ration book, considering that she was almost a member of the family, and one who had been bereaved at that?

'What are your plans now, then? I suppose you have a job to go back to?'

To Ruth's dismay the girl let out a cry of anguish. 'I can't go back there! I've nowhere to go! I'm expecting

Idris's baby and my parents have thrown me out of the house. That's why I've come to Wales, you see? I thought Idris's parents might take me in because it's their grandchild, isn't it?'

'I don't know what to say,' Ruth said, shocked at this revelation. 'It's not up to me, is it? You can stay here tonight, and then we'll go to the cottage hospital tomorrow afternoon to see Dora — that's Idris's mother. It's lucky you've come today because they only have visiting hours once a week, and that's tomorrow.'

She knew that she was babbling but she'd never been in a situation like this before. One thing was certain: she couldn't turn the poor girl out on the street, as her parents had evidently done. What sort of people would do that to their own daughter anyway? Surely they'd think again after the original shock had worn off.

Lorna's meeting with Mamgu was something of an ordeal. Of course, in Mamgu's young day, the workhouse would have been the only place of refuge for a young girl in disgrace.

She looked at Lorna through narrowed eyes.

'Engaged, is it? How come Idris never mentioned you then? Wrote to his mam regular, he did, and no word of getting married.'

'It was just arranged on his last leave, Mrs Thomas. Of course, he would have broken the news in time, but he was killed first, wasn't he?'

The girl dabbed at her eyes, looking pathetic.

Another thought occurred to Mamgu. Her body might be partly crippled now but she was a shrewd old lady.

'Mr Greene said you mistook him for my son, Dai. How is it you thought that Dai might be here, then?'

'This is his home, of course. Where else would he be?'

'Where he'd be is away on his ship! Didn't Idris tell you that?'

'I expect he did, but I'd forgotten,' the girl faltered. 'This has all been such a shock to me, you see. First I found out I was expecting a baby, and then my parents told me I had to go. I've been beside myself with worry.'

Mair Thomas looked thoroughly disapproving.

'In my day you went to the chapel first to say your vows before you thought of that sort of thing! And now your parents have cast you out and you've come to us, expecting us to pick up the pieces!'

'Idris was afraid he might get killed, Mrs Thomas. I didn't think it was so very wrong to give him a bit of comfort before he went back to the war. After all, we were engaged. And as for coming here now, I thought the family might be glad to know that, even thought they've lost Idris, his child is on the way. Your great-grandchild, Mrs Thomas.'

'Hmm!' Mamgu didn't look convinced. 'Well, you'll have to wait and see what Dora has to say about this, won't you?'

Once again, poor Ruth went to the hospital as the bearer of bad news. She hoped Dora wasn't going to shoot the messenger, so to speak. Things were still a bit stiff between them as a result of Ruth's awkward handling of Dora's grief.

'You wait here,' Ruth instructed Lorna when they reached the door of the ward. 'I'd better go in first and prepare Mrs Thomas.'

Dora looked up, surprised, from the magazine she was leafing through.

'Hello, Ruth! What brings you here? I thought you weren't coming this week. You said something about a Red Cross meeting; packing comforts for the troops, wasn't it?'

'I had to give that a miss. We've got a bit of a problem at home.'

'Don't tell me Bob's got himself in a muddle with the ration books or something?'

'No, no, nothing like that. It's, well, a

young woman turned up yesterday, from Portsmouth. She says she's Idris's fiancée.'

Dora's jaw dropped.

'It's the first I've heard of him being engaged! Why would he want to keep a thing like that secret?'

'I can't answer that, Dora, but that's not all. Apparently she's expecting a baby, and Idris is the father.'

Dora screwed up her face so that the lines on her forehead and around her mouth deepened.

'This is all I need! I suppose I'd better see the girl, though, hadn't I? Where is she now?'

'Waiting outside the door,' Ruth told her.

Marina Becomes A Spy!

Lorna had been staying with the Greenes for almost a month, and tempers were becoming frayed.

Marina hated sharing her room with the older girl, not least because it was so small. More than once she'd come home from work to find Lorna's things taking up space on her bed, but when she complained, Lorna said there wasn't enough room in the wardrobe.

She'd even hinted that Marina should give up her bed!

'I get so tired now that I'm expecting. You wouldn't believe how much my back aches, and that camp bed is hopeless.'

'It's a lot better than what you'd find in the workhouse!' Marina snapped.

'There's no need to take that tone with me! When it boils down to it I have more right to be here than you do, since

I'm the mother of Idris's child. You people are only visitors here.'

These spats were becoming more frequent, but the worst of it was that Lorna didn't show her true colours to the other members of the household. She was all sweetness and light in front of everyone else, especially Bob, who felt sorry for her.

'Try to show a bit of sympathy,' he suggested, when Marina had a moan to him. 'It's not easy for her, you know, being in a mess like this. Try to imagine how you'd feel in a similar situation.'

'I wouldn't *be* in a similar situation, Dad! I'd have more sense!'

'I should jolly well hope so,' he countered.

After getting nowhere with him, Marina went to talk to her mother.

'I can't take much more of this, Mum! She's driving me up the wall! She's really nasty to me and she snaps at me all the time for no reason. She reckons that we're just interlopers, living here, and it's obvious that she can't wait for us to move out so that she can have a bedroom all to herself. Well, the feeling's mutual. Honestly Mum, I don't think I can stand to share a room with her for five more minutes.'

'I don't know what you expect me to do about it, my girl. Where else could we put her? You tell me that.'

'There's plenty of room in the parlour, Mum.'

'What, put her in with Mamgu? I don't think so. You may not have noticed, but Mamgu has taken a violent dislike to Miss Lorna Pearson.'

'Then somebody round here has seen sense,' Marina mumbled. 'I wish we could go back to Hemel. I can't wait for the day!'

'Can't you, love?' Ruth spoke slyly and her daughter reddened.

Returning to England would mean saying goodbye to Tim Parry, and Ruth had a pretty good idea of the way the wind was blowing.

Poor old Bob still thought his

255

daughter was going out with a group of young friends, with Tim accompanying them as a sort of minder. He had no idea that Marina and Tim had become a twosome.

Ruth had been against this at first, with Tim being older and more worldly wise, but she knew she had to cut the apron strings sooner or later, so for now she was turning a blind eye.

In a way it was good that Lorna was here; her presence would serve as an awful warning to Marina in case she was ever in danger of getting carried away.

Even so, it wouldn't do any harm to have a little chat about the situation with Dora, she thought, when she next went to see her at the cottage hospital.

'Look at you!' she exclaimed, when she entered the ward and approached her cousin's bed. 'How does it feel to have both your legs down flat?'

'Wonderful! I can turn over on my side at last, and what's more, I can scratch my leg now they've taken the plaster cast off. How are things at home?'

'A bit fraught, I'm afraid.'

'The effect of having a little cuckoo in the nest, I suppose?'

'Exactly.'

'It'll be even more difficult once I come home. I'll be having physio-therapy for a bit, of course, but I can't wait to get out of here. You've all been so good, and I don't want to impose on you any longer than I have to, but I was hoping that you could stay on with us for a bit. I wouldn't mind sharing with Mamgu, and with her room being on the ground floor I wouldn't have to tackle the stairs. Still, it will be a full house, won't it?'

'Have you thought about letting Lorna stay after we've gone back to Hemel? She could help you around the house — perhaps even serve in the shop? I can't say she's proved very willing up to now, but perhaps she'd be different with you. According to Marina the girl seems to regard us as interlopers.'

'Cheeky madam!'

'What does she mean to do with the baby when it comes, I wonder? Has she discussed her plans with you?'

Dora shrugged. 'She mentioned having it adopted, but I don't know what the chances are of that. Most people are taking care of evacuees as it is.'

'Is that what you'd like to see happen?'

Dora sighed.

'Not really. I hate to think of my first grandchild going to strangers or ending up in an orphanage somewhere. I think Lorna would like me to take it myself, but I don't know if I'm up to taking on a baby at my age.'

'That's a bit of a cheek, isn't it, palming it off on to you? Surely it's her responsibility?'

'I know, but I keep coming back to the fact that this baby is my own flesh and blood. Idris may be gone, but he'll live on through this child. One idea going through my mind is that Lorna can stay with me and when the baby comes she can go out to work while I keep an eye on him or her. After all, I do work in my own shop. I can juggle both jobs, so to speak.'

'There's one thing you haven't mentioned,' Ruth murmured.

'What's that, then?'

'Well, her own parents. Pearson, isn't that their name? This is their grandchild, too. I know they've been very unkind, but I'm sure they were in shock when they gave the poor girl the 'never darken my door again' routine. They may be regretting it now, but can't do anything about it because they don't know where she is. I do think you should contact them, Dora. See what they have to say. If they are still dead against welcoming her back home, then you'll have to think again.'

'Oh, I've thought of it already. I've even suggested contacting her parents to Lorna herself, but she refuses to part with their address. Says it's no use. Their minds are quite made up.'

* * *

'Who's that staying in your house, Marina?' Tim wanted to know, having caught a glimpse of Lorna sunning herself on the wall at the side of the road. 'Not from round here, is she?'

'Her name's Lorna. She comes from Portsmouth.'

He whistled through his teeth. 'Think she'd go out with me if I ask her nicely?'

Marina was cut to the quick by this insensitive remark.

'I shouldn't think so,' she said, in as cold a voice as she could muster. 'She's Idris's widow. At least, they were engaged and planning to marry on his next leave. What I mean is, she's bereaved, and grieving.'

'Maybe I could cheer her up, then,' he leered. Marina wasn't sure he was serious, but she resolved to put a spoke in his wheel without delay.

'I doubt it. She's expecting a baby!' she snapped.

'Oh, well then, better not get involved,' he remarked. 'Don't want to get a bad reputation, do I?'

'Oh, no, that wouldn't do at all,' she said, fuming. She was beginning to wonder what she'd ever seen in Tim Parry. To think that she'd dreamed about him for so long, only to learn that her idol had feet of clay!

Then, one day, Marina overheard a conversation between her parents.

'Dora feels she ought to contact the Pearsons, to give them a chance to reconcile themselves with their daughter,' Ruth said.

'That certainly seems like the right course of action to me,' Bob agreed.

'The only trouble is, Dora hasn't been able to worm their address out of the girl. She keeps saying there's no point, that they don't want to know. And Portsmouth is such a big place, and Pearson is quite a common name. We thought perhaps you could try speaking to Lorna, Bob. After all, she seems to have taken quite a shine to you.'

'Count me out! This is women's stuff. I'm not getting involved, no fear!'.

Marina tiptoed softly up the stairs. Lorna was splashing about in the bath tub, using up all the hot water in the geyser. She surely wouldn't have taken her handbag in there with her, so it must be lying around in their room. Snooping through someone's private possessions was beastly, but in this case Marina thought it was justified.

Finding Lorna's home address was easy enough, as there were several documents in the bag, including her identity card, ration book, and birth certificate. In this time of air raids people kept their valuables with them at all times, and from studying Lorna's papers, Marina could see that, until now, Lorna had lived in the same house as her parents since the day she'd been born.

Grabbing a pencil and a slip of paper, Marina jotted down the address and, for good measure, the first names of the Pearsons as well. Then she returned the documents to Lorna's handbag, taking care to replace them in the pocket where she'd found them. As she did so, a photograph fell to the floor.

It showed a rather handsome young man, dressed in naval uniform. Idris, of course.

But when she turned it over, the writing on the back told a different story.

'*To my darling Lorna, all my love, always, Freddie.*'

★　★　★

Sitting up in bed, Dora glanced over some recipes in a magazine that she'd borrowed from the patient in the next bed. The one for rissoles sounded not half bad, even if the main ingredient did seem to be oatmeal. Still, you could do a lot with the addition of herbs, and she had those in her garden at home.

She looked up and saw a middle-aged couple coming into the ward. Either they were new visitors who didn't know when visiting day was, she mused, in which case it was a miracle they'd got past the ball porter, or someone in the ward was on their last legs.

The pair stopped at the desk to have a word with Sister, and they evidently passed muster because now they were headed in Dora's direction.

Dora suddenly realised who they must be and she smoothed down her hair and made sure her bed-jacket was hiding any exposed flesh which the skimpy hospital nightdress didn't cover.

'Mrs Thomas?'

'Yes, that's me.'

'I'm Edith Pearson and this is my husband, George.'

'How do you do?'

'How do you do? We're Lorna's parents, of course. We had your letter, Mrs Thomas, and we came as soon as we could. May we sit down?'

'Please do.' Dora indicated the upright wooden chair that waited beside her locker. 'Perhaps you'd like to borrow Mrs Franklin's chair, Mr Pearson?' she added, indicating her bed neighbour.

'Just you bring it back when you've finished with it, that's all!' that lady insisted. 'Somebody took it away last visitors' day, they did, and my Morgan had to stand up all afternoon like he was waiting for a bus.'

That settled, the Pearsons looked at each other and began to talk in turn, like a music hall team.

'We've been so worried ever since our girl disappeared, Mrs Thomas.'

'We've looked all over Portsmouth, but never a sign of her. Of course, we had no way of knowing she'd gone to Wales!'

'It was good of you to take her into your home, but there's something here we don't understand. Several things, actually. First of all, we knew that Lorna was engaged, but we'd never heard of your son until we got your letter.'

Dora felt it was time to get a word in.

'We knew nothing about Lorna either, Mr Pearson. I understand that the engagement came about during Idris's last leave and, well, we both know what happened soon after that. Idris had no time to write and tell us, of course.'

'We were so sorry to hear of your son's death,' Edith Pearson murmured. 'You must find it very hard to come to grips with it.'

'Thank you. I'm starting to come to terms with it now, but at first I didn't want to believe it.'

'Something we have to come to terms with is that Lorna is expecting a baby,' George Pearson said. 'Of course, these things do happen, especially in wartime, but I wish she could have confided in us instead of running away like this.'

'I don't understand,' said Dora, frowning. 'She said you did know — that was why you threw her out of the house. That's the main reason I agreed to have her with us. The poor

266

girl had nowhere else to go.'

'Is that what she told you, Mrs Thomas?' Edith's Pearson's expression was deeply shocked. 'No, I'm afraid you've got the wrong end of the stick. Quite some time ago, Lorna got to know a young naval officer, called Freddie Mitchell. She brought him home to meet us and I must say, we took against him from the start. He was a real rough diamond, Mrs Thomas.

'Well, when the two of them announced they were getting engaged, we weren't pleased, I can tell you. Then George made some enquiries about the boy and discovered that he was a real bad lot. He'd been in trouble with the police. He'd also had a string of girlfriends and we felt sure he was leading our girl up the garden path.'

Edith Pearson sighed, and turned to look at her husband, who took up the story.

'I told Lorna that we wouldn't stand to have a son-in-law like him in the family, and that she'd have to break it off with him. Well, it's all water under the bridge now, because the lad went down with his ship, as it happens. But at the time of the argument, Lorna got really upset at us and stormed off, out of the house. I can only think she must have broken off with Freddie and taken up with your Idris somewhere along the way, because we've heard nothing of her since, until we got your letter.'

'So, what are you going to do?' Dora asked.

'We'll take her home with us, today, if you'll be good enough to give us directions to find your home.'

'That's good, but what I really meant was, what about the baby?'

'That's something we'll have to work out with Lorna, Mrs Thomas.'

'But please don't forget that he or she is my grandchild,' Dora pleaded.

'We'll be in touch,' Edith promised.

After they'd left, Dora fell back upon her pillows, savouring the moment.

Until now she hadn't realised just how much stress she'd been under, feeling responsible for the girl.

She began to feel really rather cross about the whole thing, too. They had all been taken in by that young minx and her tale of cruel parents. But by the sound of it, her parents were quite ready to swallow their disappointment and stand by her, so why had she come all the way to Wales with her sob story?

Could she have meant to get money out of them or something? She had already lived at their expense for quite some time!

★ ★ ★

Once again, Bob, on duty in the shop, was the first to know what was happening. This time he was addressed by his proper name, and George Pearson explained that he and his wife had come directly from the hospital where they had spoken to Dora.

'Is our daughter here, Mr Greene? We've come to take her home.'

'My wife told me that Dora was

269

going to write to you,' Bob said. 'I'm glad you had a change of heart, Mr Pearson. Lorna is your daughter, no matter what she's done.'

For the second time that day, the Pearsons had to tell their side of the story.

Not surprisingly, Lorna was none too pleased to see her parents.

The usual ritual of tea and explanations disposed of, the Pearsons prepared to leave.

'Say thank you to Mrs Greene,' Edith prompted.

'Thank you for having me, Mrs Greene,' Lorna murmured, like a child who was leaving a not particularly enjoyable birthday party.

'Goodbye and good riddance to bad rubbish,' Mamgu muttered, when the door had closed behind their unwelcome guest.

'That's a bit harsh, isn't?' Bob remonstrated.

'Not a bit of it, Mr Greene. I didn't take to her from the first. Her eyes are

270

set too close together.'

Ruth laughed. 'We can't help our looks, Mrs Thomas. The girl does have good taste, at least; she chose your grandson, didn't she? And she is going to give you your first great-grandchild, which is something in her favour.'

'I didn't ask her to,' Mamgu grumbled. 'And now look what's happened. The *baban* growing up without a dada.'

★ ★ ★

'I'm glad that's all over,' Ruth told her husband, as he took the camp bed apart and she gathered up the bedding to await wash-day Monday. 'Let's hope everything goes well from here on. Dora will be coming home soon, so that's something to look forward to.'

'I suppose that means we'll be heading home ourselves one of these days. Should I write to old Pete and see about getting the house back?'

'Perhaps not yet, dear. Dora did say something about our staying on for a bit. She won't be back to normal just yet, after all that time in hospital.'

Marina was delighted when she heard that Lorna had gone.

'Thank goodness for that! Wasn't it clever of Auntie Dora to talk her parents round?'

'From what they told us, I don't think she needed to. They were very worried when she disappeared and were immensely relieved when they had Dora's letter.'

'But they chucked her out when they found out she was expecting!'

'Apparently not. They knew nothing about that. They did have a row ages ago when a chap she'd been seeing turned out to be a bad lot and some harsh words were said.'

'Freddie somebody?' Marina cried.

'How did you know about that? Did Lorna tell you?'

'She carries a photo of him in her bag, Mum. His name is written on the back.'

'She can't have known Idris very

long, then. She probably fell for him on the rebound. Well, the poor girl's been doubly bereaved now. That other chap was lost at sea, too.'

Marina was glad now that she'd said nothing to Lorna or Ruth about that photo. What a thing to happen. She could imagine nothing worse than falling in love with a man who turned out to be a rotter.

After a moment's pause, she realised that of course she could imagine something worse, and that was falling in love with someone who went away to war and got himself killed.

A Miracle!

Marina was alone in the house. It was her day off and she was determined to enjoy it to the full, but the trouble was that she couldn't think of anything exciting to do and had no one to do it with anyway.

Marged was at work because they were on different shifts; they hardly ever saw each other any more.

Tim was also at work. Marina tried to imagine him crawling along, far below the surface of the earth, and failed. Or could it be that she was no longer really interested in him? He was beginning to bore her. Catrin Harris could have him back and welcome.

It was early closing day and Marina's parents had gone out for a walk, Ruth saying that she wanted to pick some hips and haws to display in the house. Dora was expected home the next day and the house had been cleaned from top to bottom to welcome her.

Basil was also out, at school, and Mamgu was having her afternoon nap, worn out with the excitement of looking forward to her daughter-in-law's return. Although she was usually quiet, old Mrs Thomas had more or less talked herself to a standstill in the past few days, directing Ruth to fetch this here and to put that there.

When the back door opened and the most gorgeous young man stood framed in the doorway, Marina was about to tell him off for walking into the house without knocking, but she found it hard to get her breath. For a moment, she felt quite light-headed. Once again it was love at first sight.

'Who are *you*?' she said at last.

'I'm Idris. Who are *you*?'

'Idris? But you're dead!' Marina's hand flew to her mouth. 'I mean, that is, if you're Idris Thomas!'

'Of course I'm Idris Thomas! But you haven't answered *my* question.'

'I'm your cousin, Marina Greene,' she said faintly. 'We've been staying here while Auntie Dora — your mum — has been in hospital.'

What on earth was going on? How could this possibly be Idris?

'Honestly, we all thought you were dead,' she stammered again.

'That was a mistake, *bach*. I got a bit too close to the pearly gates, but my number wasn't up and they sent me back again. So here I am, turning up like a bad penny!'

'I can't take it in. They're planning to hold a memorial service for you at the chapel! They would have done it sooner if Auntie Dora hadn't been in the hospital. She's coming home tomorrow, as it happens.'

'Look, you must have got my telegram!' he told her. 'Sent days ago, it was. I came as soon as I could, expecting to have the fatted calf killed for me, and now this. And you say nobody knows a thing about it?'

'You may have to make do with a

couple of sausages!' Marina was slowly recovering her equilibrium. 'Meat is on the ration, in case you hadn't heard!'

He nodded. 'Put the kettle on, then, *bach*, while I bring in my kit bag.'

In a daze, she did as she was asked. Obviously there was a story to be told, but there was no point in asking about it until Mum and Dad returned as he would only have to repeat it all to them.

'Good cup of tea, that,' he said, smiling, once they were sitting at the table, looking at each other with growing interest. 'Any more in the pot? And where have you hidden Mamgu? How is she?'

'She sleeps in the parlour now. In fact, she should be waking up from her nap at any moment. Shall I go and break the news to her?'

'Oh, no, I think that's my job, don't you?'

He got up and put his head round the parlour door.

'Time to wake up, Mamgu, unless you mean to sleep the whole day!'

The old lady stared at her grandson in astonishment. Then she held out her arms and Idris went to her, kneeling down on the floor at her bedside so he could share her embrace.

Marina stood in the doorway, watching them. They were speaking Welsh now, and she couldn't understand a word of it. However, it didn't take a knowledge of the ancient Celtic language to know what was going on.

Tears of joy were rolling down Mamgu's wrinkled cheeks as she held Idris's face in her hands. She seemed to be asking question after question and not getting any answers.

Marina wasn't needed here. She tiptoed away in time to hear her parents arriving back from their walk.

'What's that thing doing here?' Bob demanded, kicking the kit bag which was lying just inside the door. 'I could have tripped over that and broken my neck!'

'Oh, is it young Ifor, home on leave' Ruth smiled. 'Dora will be so happy

278

see the boy when she finds him waiting to greet her!'

'She'll be happy, all right, Mum, but it isn't Ifor who's come home. It's Idris!'

'Idris! Don't be so silly, Marina. What a thing to say! And not in very good taste, either, I'm sorry to say.'

'Hello, Auntie Ruth!' Idris appeared in the doorway, grinning.

Ruth's hands flew to her mouth.

'Well, I never did!'

She and her husband seemed to be frozen in place.

Bob recovered first. 'Idris, lad! This is wonderful! But where have you been all this time, and where have you come from now?'

'Not heaven, obviously. Look, I'm dying for a bath. Is there any hot water? We'll all sit down together after tea and I'll tell you all about it then.'

'This is the most wonderful news, of course,' Ruth muttered, when Idris had disappeared upstairs, 'but I do think he might have let us know. Him turning up like this could have given Mamgu another stroke.'

'I don't think you need worry about her, Mum. She was overjoyed, of course, but funnily enough Idris's sudden appearance didn't seem to come as a shock. And anyway, he says he did send a telegram.'

'Well, I certainly didn't see any telegram coming here,' Bob said.

'I bet I know what happened,' Marina said. 'Remember that letter from the Inland Revenue that was sent on from Hemel? I bet you . . . '

There was no letter-box in the shop door, and the elderly postman usually stepped inside to deliver the post. If the shop happened to be closed, he pushed the letters under the door. The tax envelope had gone under the mat and hadn't been discovered until Ruth had moved it to sweep up.

Marina darted into the shop and, sure enough, there was an orange envelope waiting to be discovered. Telegrams were supposed to be handed to the recipient in case there was a reply to be sent, but this one had probably come when nobody was about and the boy had wanted to get rid of it.

'He should be reported,' Bob grunted.

'Whose kit bag is that? What's it doing here?' Basil had come home from school, looking as if a whirlwind had struck him. His tie was unknotted, his shoelaces were trailing on the floor and he seemed to be covered in dust.

'Go into the scullery and wash your face and hands, Basil. Tea will be on the table shortly!' Ruth directed.

'And tuck your shirt in, too!' Bob ordered. 'You're not coming to the table looking like that, my boy.'

At that moment Idris came down the stairs, looking very smart. He had put his uniform back on after his bath, and Marina wondered if this was because he had no civilian clothes to wear, or if there was something in the rules which said he had to dress that way.

Basil was enthralled by the sight.

'Cor! Are you in the Navy, mister? Were you a friend of my cousin Idris? He was a hero, you know. He went down with his ship.'

'I don't know about being a hero, boyo, but *I'm* Idris, see? And as you can see, I didn't drown when the ship went down.'

'Cor!' Basil said again. Just wait until school tomorrow. He'd be the centre of attention all right, with this tale to tell.

When tea was over, Idris leaned back in his chair and unfolded his story. In deference to the women present he said little about the terror of that night; of the death and destruction that was all around the crew of his ship when it was torpedoed; of the plunge into the dark, icy waters, and the stress-filled hours that followed as they waited in their over-filled lifeboats for rescue.

'We were picked up by another British ship, but that was sunk too, not long afterwards. In that second attack I was knocked out cold. Presumably I was put into one of the lifeboats along with the rest, and eventually transported to hospital. I was unconscious for days and the nurses told me later that they had no idea who I was. I'd lost all my belongings, of course, and they had no means of identifying me.'

'But surely some of your shipmates knew who you were?'

'We were separated in all the confusion, Uncle Bob. I suspect that all those in the lifeboat with me were men from the other ship, the one that rescued us from the second attack. As I found out later, hundreds were lost that night, and I imagine the authorities believed I was among them. It wasn't until I came back to my senses that I was able to explain who I was.'

*   *   *

The next day, Dora came home to a flurry of excitement. The whole family was crowded into the doorway when the ambulance drew up, and Dora was helped down by the uniformed attendants. Aided by a walking stick, she made her way slowly to the house.

She and Ruth kissed the air above each other's cheeks as the rest of the family stood by, beaming.

'Someone's here to see you, Auntie Dora! Somebody really special!'

Basil had been warned to keep quiet about the surprise which awaited her, but he'd been unable to contain his excitement and blurted this out.

Dora clasped her hands together, dropping her stick in the process

'It's Ifor, isn't it? They've given him leave so he can welcome me home.'

There was no stopping Basil now.

'No, it's not Ifor! Guess who it is, Auntie, guess!'

'Don't tell me it's my Dai!'

'Oh, better than that, Auntie!'

'Nothing on earth could be better than that at this moment, Basil love.'

'Yes, it could! Yes, it could!'

'What do you say then, Mam?' Idris stepped out of the parlour.

After a moment of stunned silence, Dora began to sob, and tears ran down the faces of all those who stood watching as she ran towards her son. Ruth said later that nobody would ever have imagined that her cousin had just come out of hospital after months of suffering with a broken leg.

A bird on the wing could not have flown any faster, she insisted.

Loose Ends

During the next few days there was a steady stream of visitors to the Thomas household as friends came to shake Idris by the hand, rejoicing in his survival.

Others came to welcome Dora home.

Mamgu kept a permanent smile on her face, and who could blame her?

'She keeps me awake half the night, telling me what a miracle it is that Idris is alive,' Dora told Ruth. 'Mind you, I'm more than happy to put up with it! I've written to tell Dai, of course, although goodness knows when he'll receive my letter.'

'What about Ifor, then? Have you written to him?'

'Of course. Oh, I do wish that both Dai and Ifor could get leave to come home and celebrate with us, but it's no good wishing for the moon! Just as well, in a way, because I don't know where we'd put them.'

Marina had volunteered to give up her room, which after all belonged to Idris by right, but he'd refused, moving in with Basil.

Needless to say, Basil was absolutely delighted to be sharing with his hero, and plagued him with questions.

Idris was very patient with the boy, answering in a kindly fashion but toning down his responses because of the child's age. In any case he preferred not to think too deeply about what he had experienced. Terrible images flooded into his mind every time he closed his eyes to go to sleep.

'I'm going to join the Navy when I grow up!' Basil enthused.

'That's nice, dear,' Ruth murmured, thinking, 'Not if I've got anything to do with it!' Still, he would probably have changed his mind by the time he reached his teens. Only last week he'd wanted to be an engine driver.

Dora was overjoyed because Idris was

to be given a shore job, at least for the time being. Despite his robust appearance the doctors had decreed that, after his terrible ordeal, he wasn't well enough to return to sea.

Something which didn't go unnoticed by their mothers was the fact that Marina and Idris were becoming increasingly drawn to each other.

'Wouldn't it be nice if they made a match of it?' Dora whispered to Ruth one evening, when the two young people were laughing over a game of Beggar My Neighbour.

'They're cousins,' Ruth countered.

'Second cousins! Anyway, cousins marry all the time, don't they?'

'Marina is much too young to think about that sort of thing.'

'She's almost seventeen!'

'Don't be so silly, Dora. When Idris goes back to wherever they send him, they'll forget all about each other.'

Dora wasn't so sure. Neither was Tim Parry.

'You don't seem to have time for me

these days,' he grumbled. 'Always hanging around that cousin of yours, you are!'

'We all thought he was dead, Tim! We're just thrilled to have him back, that's all.'

Tim glowered at her. 'Is that all?'

'Of course. Look, if you're feeling left out, why don't you come and join us? I'm sure Idris would love to see you.'

'I might ask Catrin to come to the pictures with me,' he countered.

'That sounds like a good idea, Tim. Or maybe you'd like us to make up a foursome?'

He shrugged. That didn't sound like a good idea to him. Catrin might fall all over the conquering hero as well. How could he compete with that?

* * *

'Will you write to me after I go back?' Idris asked Marina, when his leave was almost up.

'Of course I will!'

She was thrilled that he'd asked, but there was something which had to be settled first. She bit her lip, wondering how to bring up the subject.

'What's the matter, *cariad*? Something wrong?'

'I was just thinking that Lorna might not like it.'

'Lorna? Who's she?'

Marina frowned. 'Your fiancée, of course!'

Now it was Idris's turn to look blank. 'What are you talking about? I'm not engaged, never have been. I don't have a fiancée.'

'But if she's having your baby you'll have to marry her, won't you, to give the child a name?'

'Is this some kind of joke?' Idris was angry now. 'I don't know what you're accusing me of, Marina, but I don't find this amusing, see.'

They were sitting out on the back step with the kitchen door open behind them. Marina heard hesitant footsteps which told her that her aunt was nearby.

'Auntie Dora!' she called. 'Could you come out here for a moment, please?' She turned back to face Idris. 'If you won't listen to me then you'd better hear what your mother has to say.'

'What is it, dear?' Dora limped outside and stood leaning on her walking stick.

'We've just been talking about Lorna Pearson,' Marina began.

'You mean *you* have!' Idris interrupted angrily. 'Do you know what this is about, Mam?'

'Oh, dear! I knew this had to be discussed sooner or later, but I've put off saying anything about it to you because I didn't want to spoil your leave.'

'What is all this, Mam? I don't know any Lorna Pearson!'

'I have to sit down, son. Can we all go inside?'

When they were seated, Dora took up the story.

'This young woman turned up here from Portsmouth after reading your name in the casualty lists. She said that the pair of you had become engaged during your last leave, and that you planned to marry in the near future. Then, when she found that she was pregnant with your baby, her parents turned her out of the house.'

'So having nowhere else to go,' Marina continued, 'she came here, thinking that we'd look after her. That the Thomas family would, I mean. She didn't know about us staying here.'

'I can't believe this!' Idris scratched his chin, beginning to look more puzzled than angry. 'Where is she now, this Lorna Pearson?'

'Back with her parents,' his mother told him. 'We managed to trace them and they came down to Wales to take her back with them. The odd thing is that they knew nothing about the expected baby, and neither had they thrown her out of their home. There had been a falling out between the girl and her father, but that had something to do with her getting engaged to a no-good rascal. From what was said, we assumed she'd given him up and started seeing you instead. It all seemed a bit sudden to me, but people do have these whirlwind romances in war time, of course.'

'A no-good rascal, you say? I wonder who he was?'

'I think I know,' Marina told him. 'She carried a photo around with her. I wish I had it here to show you. His name was on the back; Freddie. I think his name was Freddie Mitchell, or something like that.'

'I knew him! We both hung around with the same crowd during the time we were in Portsmouth. I'm sorry to hear that he's been killed, but it's true that he was no good. There was a lot of talk about his bragging about all the girls he'd led up the garden path.'

'I see what happened!' Marina cried, her eyes sparkling. 'Freddie got engaged to Lorna — with no intention of marrying her — and when she learned she was expecting his baby, he said he wanted nothing more to do with her. She was desperate, so she looked through the casualty lists to find someone who had also been in Portsmouth at the right time. Then she turned up here to take advantage of your family!'

Idris threw back his head and laughed. 'My goodness, *cariad!* What sort of books have you been reading?'

Marina blushed, but she stuck to her story. 'I can't make you believe me, Idris, but just tell me why else would she'd come here posing as your fiancée if you've never heard of her before?'

'Marina's right so far as that goes,' Dora said, nodding. 'Oh, the first part of your idea is just supposition, dear. But we can't deny what happened after she arrived here. She was quite convincing, Idris. I even thought of letting her stay on, and helping her to bring up the baby — my grandchild, as I believed — but then the Pearsons came and took charge of her. Now, of course, I know it was all a confidence trick. Perhaps she'd have tried to get money out of me, or even gone off after the baby came, leaving it with me like a little cuckoo in the nest!'

'For all she knew I could have been married.' Idris had no choice but to accept the story now.

'Easy enough to find out your circumstances if she went to the authorities, claiming that she'd had a relationship with you,' Dora said.

'I'll have to sort all this out when I return to Portsmouth, Mam. That young woman is going to get a shock, in more ways than one!'

Time To Go Home

'We'll be home for Christmas!' Basil carolled joyfully. 'I can't wait!'

'Do you mean you can't wait for Christmas, or you can't wait to go back to your own house?' Dora smiled.

'Both! I don't like it here.' Catching sight of his mother's frown, he hastily changed his tune. 'Sorry, Auntie Dora! I don't mean I don't like your house, or staying with you; only that some not very nice things have happened to me since I came here.'

'Rhodri, I suppose. Well, I can't say I blame you. He's been very unkind and badly behaved, by all accounts.'

'I'll miss Mr Rees, though. He's nice. If I'd stayed, I could have helped him plant his garden next spring.'

'Never mind, you can come back to visit one of these days, and you'll see him then.'

'Well, I've thoroughly enjoyed being here.' Bob beamed. 'Running a shop is right up my alley. I was saying to Ruth that I'd like to get a little place of our own after the war. A tobacconist's and sweet shop, perhaps.'

'What will you do in the meantime, though? You wouldn't think of going back to your own trade, I suppose?'

'Not if the doctor has anything to do with it. No, I'll see if I can get a job serving in a shop somewhere in Hemel. I feel I have the experience to manage one, but we'll have to see. If there aren't any vacancies for managers then I'll work as a shop assistant to tide us over.'

'Make sure it's in a sweet shop, Dad!' Basil piped up, making everyone smile.

'And Marina will have to see what's available for her, now that she's joined the ranks of the world's workers,' Bob remarked.

'Ah, well, Bob, I've been thinking about that. Marina has a good job here, and she's settled in nicely. What would you think of her staying on with me?

I'm still a bit below par, and she'd be a help to me in the house.'

'Well, I don't know; she's a bit young to be leaving home.'

'Leaving home, my foot! She'll be with her family here, and I'll keep an eye on her.'

Bob was still not convinced. 'You'd need to keep an eye on her, Dora. I'm beginning to think there's something going on between her and that young Parry chap. They're not sweethearts, are they?'

He looked round in surprise as his wife and her cousin groaned.

'You're behind the times, Bob Greene!'

'What's that, love?'

'Never mind,' Ruth sighed.

Marina was in seventh heaven. She'd had a letter from Idris, to say that he'd called on the Pearsons and had an awkward interview with Lorna and her father.

Pearson had been belligerent at first, but then Lorna had broken down and admitted what she'd done. Her poor father hadn't known where to look. He'd apologised profusely and kept saying that he didn't understand how she could have behaved the way she had. That wasn't the way she'd been brought up.

In floods of tears, Lorna had told Idris and her parents what had really happened, although Idris did wonder if they were crocodile tears. She'd already shown herself to be untruthful, so what was one more lie?

But it seemed that Marina's theory had been quite correct. Lorna had continued to see the disreputable Freddie until, to her horror, she'd discovered that she was pregnant. She'd told him about it, expecting him to stand by her, but instead he'd shrugged her off, asking her what she expected him to do about it. He'd even questioned whether the child was really his.

And next thing, he'd been killed in action.

'*That was when she thought of me,*'

wrote Idris. 'Apparently we had mutual acquaintances, and it was from them that she heard that I'd also been killed, as was thought at the time. Her nasty little scheme just grew from there.'

After writing on more general topics, Idris finished the letter by saying one or two things which brought tears of happiness to Marina's eyes.

They were too personal to share here, but it's enough to say that love will flourish, war or no war, and when Bob, Ruth and Basil went back to England, and Tim went back to Catrin, Marina stayed behind at the little shop in Bedwen, confident in the knowledge that Idris really was her knight in shining armour.

THE END

We do hope that you have enjoyed reading this large print book.

Did you know that all of our titles are available for purchase?

We publish a wide range of high quality large print books including:
Romances, Mysteries, Classics
General Fiction
Non Fiction and Westerns

Special interest titles available in large print are:
The Little Oxford Dictionary
Music Book, Song Book
Hymn Book, Service Book

Also available from us courtesy of Oxford University Press:
Young Readers' Dictionary
(large print edition)
Young Readers' Thesaurus
(large print edition)

For further information or a free brochure, please contact us at:
Ulverscroft Large Print Books Ltd.,
The Green, Bradgate Road, Anstey,
Leicester, LE7 7FU, England.
Tel: (00 44) **0116 236 4325**
Fax: (00 44) **0116 234 0205**

TO LOVE AGAIN

Catriona McCuaig

Jenny Doyle had always loved her brother in law, Jake Thomas-Harding, but when he chose to marry her sister instead, she knew it was a love that had no future. Now his wife is dead, and he asks Jenny to live under his roof to look after his little daughter. She wonders what the future holds for them all, especially when ghosts of the past arise to haunt them . . .

FINDING THE SNOWDON LILY

Heather Pardoe

Catrin Owen's father, a guide on Snowdon, shows botanists the sites of rare plants. He wants his daughter to marry Taran Davies. But then the attractive photographer Philip Meredith and his sister arrive, competing to be first to photograph the 'Snowdon Lily' in its secret location. His arrival soon has Catrin embroiled in the race, and she finds her life, as well as her heart, at stake. For the coveted prize generates treachery amongst the rivals — and Taran's jealousy . . .

KEEP SAFE THE PAST

Dorothy Taylor

Their bookshop in the old Edwardian Arcade meant everything to Jenny Wyatt and her father. But were the rumours that the arcade was to be sold to a development company true? Jenny decides to organise a protest group. Then, when darkly attractive Leo Cooper enters her life, his upbeat personality is like a breath of fresh air. But as their relationship develops, Jenny questions her judgement of him. Are her dreams of true love about to be dashed?

LEGACY OF REGRET

Jo James

When Liz Shepherd unexpectedly inherits an elderly man's considerable estate, she is persuaded it is in gratitude for her kindness to him. But doubts set in when Steve Lewis, in the guise of a reporter, challenges her good luck. Was there another reason for her legacy? And why is Steve so interested? She comes to regret her inheritance and all its uncertainties — until Steve helps her find the truth and they discover the secret of their past.

RETURN TO
HEATHERCOTE MILL

Jean M. Long

Annis had vowed never to set foot in Heathercote Mill again. It held too many memories of her ex-fiancé, Andrew Freeman, who had died so tragically. But now her friend Sally was in trouble, and desperate for Annis' help with her wedding business. Reluctantly, Annis returned to Heathercote Mill and discovered many changes had occurred during her absence. She found herself confronted with an entirely new set of problems — not the least of them being Andrew's cousin, Ross Hadley . . .